"You don't even know me."

Silence.

Just when she thought she'd gotten through to him, that he was going to let her leave, his voice came as a soft, sensual caress. Dark, like chocolate, and just as tempting.

"I know it's crazy, but there's a part of me that feels like I've known you forever. Like I've been waiting for you. There's something between us, don't deny it. I know you feel it, too."

She sucked in a sharp breath. Yes, she did feel it. She hadn't realized *he* did. It was crazy and unexpected, but it was there. A connection apparently neither could deny. It terrified her even as it thrilled her. Unfortunately, this whole thing made her situation that much harder.

"Talk to me, Kayla," he whispered in her ear. "Let me help you."

Whatever powers that be—God, the Universe, or Aliens—that had led her to this man, they knew there was a reason she needed to meet him now, at this point in her life.

Maybe he wouldn't turn her in. Maybe he would be the one to help her. David may be a cop...but so was Ryder. Could he help her find evidence to prove her innocence? That was his job, after all, solving crimes. Maybe she *could* trust him. Trust this insane feeling she got whenever he was near.

Taking a deep, shaky breath, and a giant leap of faith, she stepped out of his arms and turned, staring directly into those intelligent, warm eyes. "My name is Kayla Jenkins, and I'm wanted by the Chicago Police Department for the murder of my roommate."

Other Mariah Ankenman titles
in the Peak Town Colorado series
available from The Wild Rose Press, Inc.:
LOVE ON THE SWEET SIDE
LOVE ON THE WILD SIDE

Love on the Risky Side

by

Mariah Ankenman

Peak Town Colorado, Book 3

This is a work of fiction. Names, characters, places, and incidents are either the product of the author's imagination or are used fictitiously, and any resemblance to actual persons living or dead, business establishments, events, or locales, is entirely coincidental.

Love on the Risky Side

COPYRIGHT © 2017 by Mariah Ankenman

Cover Art by *Kristian Norris*

The Wild Rose Press, Inc.
PO Box 708
Adams Basin, NY 14410-0708
Visit us at www.thewildrosepress.com

Publishing History
First Yellow Rose Edition, 2017
Print ISBN 978-1-5092-1566-9
Digital ISBN 978-1-5092-1567-6

Peak Town Colorado, Book 3
Published in the United States of America

Dedications

For Ms. Cohu,
thanks for encouraging the dreams of a nine-year-old.
~*~
To all the teachers out there
shaping young minds and lives, thank you.
You do amazing work for so little thanks.
~*~
And to my Prince Charming.
Thank you for letting me bounce ideas off you
even at two a.m.

Chapter 1

Where in the world am I?

Kayla Jenkins stumbled through the dark, snowy woods. A cold wind whipped around her, like shards of glass slicing her face.

Damn, and I thought Chicago was freezing. Wherever the heck she was, it could give the Illinois winter a run for its money.

She hunched deeper into her large winter parka. Thank God it had been in her car when she ran. With David chasing her, her only thought had been to get away. She'd been all the way downtown before she realized she was still covered in vomit and blood. Thankfully, she always kept some moist wipes in her glove box. Not as good as a shower, but a quick pull into an alley and at least the worst of the mess was cleaned.

Her shirt had been a total loss. She had ditched it in the nearest dumpster and continued on in only her bra and coat, knowing it wouldn't be long before David called his boss, the police chief. Luckily, she'd been able to find a cheap replacement T-shirt at a convenience store. The thin cotton garment was not as nice as her silk blouse, but beggars couldn't be choosers.

She'd had no choice but to disappear.

After ditching her car and pulling as much cash as

she could from her bank account, she hurried to the nearest bus station and bought a ticket to the farthest destination they had. Some town in Kansas whose name she couldn't remember.

Burning cold pricks of pain shot through her foot as she tripped over a rock or stump—who could tell in all this snow—and her mouth opened with a loud shriek. She paused, leaning against a tree to catch her breath. Wincing, she squeezed her eyes shut, trying to block out the physical and emotional pain overwhelming her.

The events of the past twenty-four hours played like a horror movie in her mind. She'd traveled through the night, a night in which she didn't sleep. Every time she closed her eyes, she saw Jen's lifeless body lying on the ground in a pool of blood. It had taken all her willpower not to break down and sob on the bus. An action which would have drawn unwanted attention she couldn't afford. So, she stayed awake and tried to formulate a plan.

When the bus arrived in Whereversville, Kansas early in the morning, she'd stood in the decrepit terminal, trying to decide where to go next. Her heart had jumped up to her throat as she glanced at the flashing news bulletin on a small, old, tube TV hanging in the corner.

"I—I tried to save her, but it was too late." There, in faded color, stood David Tyler, looking mournful as he spoke to the reporter. "Jennifer was such a sweet woman. We loved each other. We were talking about getting married and starting a family." He paused as if composing himself. "I know Kayla was always a little jealous of Jen, but I never thought she'd take it this far."

What a liar!

He was spouting his ridiculous story to every news station that would listen. And they were all lapping it up like dogs. She wouldn't have a chance at proving her innocence.

"Kayla," David said directly to the camera...

Her breath had stopped. Stupid, he couldn't actually see her. But his dark gaze had focused like he was in the small bus station with her. Her blood ran cold as his harsh voice spoke over the television. She always felt the guy was kind of a jerk, but gave him the benefit of a doubt because Jen liked him.

He turned out to be far worse than she ever imagined.

"I know you're out there somewhere," he continued. "How could you do this to Jen?"

I didn't do it! You *did!*

"She loved you, and this is how you repay her?" A sob broke from beside David. He reached out an arm, placing it around Carla Wright, Jen's mother. Her father was there, too, eyes red from crying, face set in stern, determined lines. Both looked destroyed.

Bile still rose in her throat, sickness and fury fighting a battle for supremacy in her stomach. Of course they were destroyed, their only child had been murdered, and they thought her best friend had done it.

Kayla had watched David rub Mrs. Wright's back in a comforting manner and wondered what the older woman would think if she knew she was being consoled by her daughter's *real* killer.

"We will find you, Kayla." His eyes hardened, gaze coming through the screen to bore into her, threating retribution. "And you *will* face the consequences of what you've done."

No, they wouldn't find her. She planned to run...and pray she found a way to reveal all of David's lies.

After the big liar finished talking, the news had flashed a picture of her on the screen with her personal information: height, weight, hair, and eye color.

Her heartbeat had raced as she glanced around the station, hunching deeper into her coat to see if anyone recognized her. But, thankfully, there'd only been a few people around that early in the morning. She quickly realized she couldn't take the bus anymore. Too public. Too many chances to be seen.

A sharp wind blew a strand of dark hair in her face, pulling her back to her current predicament—being lost and cold. She automatically went to tie the length back, then remembered she'd chopped off her long, coppery locks. A tear slipped down her cheek, burning a frozen path on her face. The short, dull brown hair had been necessary. No reason to cry over cut and dyed hair...but she'd loved her hair. She'd had to do something to change her appearance, as much as she could, anyway. But, she was a kindergarten teacher for goodness sake, not an international spy.

Then there was the hitchhiking. The first trucker had been nice, but the second...

A shudder racked her body. Her skin still crawled remembering how he demanded *payment* for the ride.

No way buddy. I'd rather walk.

That was how she ended up in these cold, snowy woods, freezing her butt off with no idea where she was.

Another strong gust whipped through the air, and she muffled out a cry of pain. *Holy cow, that hurts. What is this wind made of, razorblades?*

Her pumps were soaked. Her poor little toes were tiny icicles on the end of frozen feet. Sensible teaching shoes were not the best footwear for snow, but it wasn't like she'd had time to change when running for her life.

The hopelessness of her situation sank in. Being blamed for a crime she didn't commit, all alone in the freezing wilderness, no idea how to help herself…

Maybe I should give it all up, lay down, and let the snow turn me into a human popsicle.

No. She couldn't give up—then David would get away with what he did to Jen.

The burn of anger briefly cut the chill. No matter what happened to her, Kayla could not let that happen. She would fight. For Jen, her friend, roommate, sister she never had. She *would* fight. Somehow, someway, she would find proof of her innocence and show the world the monster David Tyler truly was.

The soft sound of crunching snow hit her ears. Standing still as stone, she glanced around the dark woods. What was out there? A bear?

No, bears hibernated during the winter, right?

She hoped so. A city girl through and through, the closest she had ever come to a bear was last year's field trip to the Lincoln Park Zoo, and she wanted to keep it that way.

Squinting into the dark, she saw a large shape coming toward her. Too big to be a bear. Her sleep-deprived brain immediately conjured up images of Bigfoot. Bigfoot lived in the woods.

Oh no, I've discovered Bigfoot, and he's going to

eat me!

As the shape came closer, she realized it wasn't Bigfoot—*because he doesn't exist*—she reminded herself. It was also not a bear. Her vision finally focused on a large gray horse. Not only a horse, but a rider, too.

The clouds in the night sky dissipated, allowing the moonlight to shine down into the woods. Kayla's heart skipped a beat as the two towered over her.

The man sat upon the horse like a warrior of olden days. Long, dark hair fluttered about his face in the wind—sharp, high cheekbones, a smooth, square jawline, and thick, dark brows pressed down over a pair of deep, warm brown eyes.

"Hello."

His voice rumbled over her like a warm blanket. What she wouldn't give for a warm blanket right now.

"Do you need some help?"

She hesitated at his question, staring into his eyes. They looked so kind and trusting, but a man's eyes had deceived her before. Until two days ago, David's eyes had always been normal; sure, the guy had given off the jerkwad vibe at times, but she never suspected the evil hidden behind those eyes. Was this man the same? Could she trust those eyes?

Did she really have a choice?

No. She had no idea where she was and was literally freezing. Yes, she needed help. The only question, would this man be her salvation...or her downfall?

Chapter 2

"Do you need some help?"

Jake Ryder watched the woman contemplate his question. Didn't seem like a difficult thing to answer—yes or no. Judging by her red nose, chapped lips, wary expression, and the fact she stood in the middle of the woods at ten in the evening, he'd guess the answer to be yes.

"Miss?" he spoke a little louder when she didn't answer.

Maybe she didn't speak English. That would stink. He never took any foreign languages in school. He knew some basic Spanish and a few Ute words, but sadly, like most Americans, he was monolingual.

"Do you speak English?"

Her wary eyes still watched him, but her lips parted, and he heard a softly whispered "Yes."

Bullet dodged there. Now, he had to figure out who she was, and what she was doing on his property.

Wind Chaser sniffed at the woman, the mare's warm breath creating a puff of steam in the cold night air. She jumped back, clearly frightened of the large Appaloosa Gray.

"No reason to be afraid, ma'am. Wind Chaser here might be huge, but she's as gentle as a puppy dog."

The woman raised a brow in disbelief.

"My name is Jake Ryder, but most folks call me

Ryder." When she didn't return the introduction, he continued. "Can I ask how you came to be all the way out here in the middle of the night?"

Giving a guarded glance from the horse back to him, she simply said, "Got lost."

And they say women were chatty. Hell, he had a pet parrot as a kid that talked more than this woman. Not a problem. As sheriff, he was used to interrogating uncooperative suspects. Not that she was a suspect, yet.

"Got lost…" He looked her over. Big, red, winter coat, long, dark slacks and—were those high heels? "…shopping?"

Honestly, who the hell wears heels in the woods?

She scowled, wrapping her arms around herself. "My car ran off the road. I—I got out to find help. Wandered off the road and got lost."

Something about her story smelled like Wind Chaser's stall after feeding time. "Why didn't you call Triple A?"

Her gaze darted to the side. "Cell died."

Yeah, and I'm the King of England.

"You need a ride back to your car?"

Her eyes widened. "On that thing?"

"*Her* name is Wind Chaser, and yes. Did you think I had a car hidden in the trees?"

Her jaw clenched at his sarcasm. Well, excuse him. It was dark, cold, and the last thing he wanted to do was be out here trying to pull a story out of Ms. Lying-Crazy-Lady.

Wind Chaser had been anxious for a good, long ride. He'd been too neglectful of his horse lately. Her pen was big enough to graze, but she needed the freedom of the woods every now and again. So, despite the cold, he'd saddled her up. Even though out longer than he'd anticipated, he hadn't expected to run into anyone out here. Especially someone who obviously needed his help, but seemed to be refusing to take it.

"I don't...know where my car is." Her nervous gaze looked everywhere but at him.

A clear sign of a lie. She better be careful or her pants were going to catch on fire.

"What road were you driving on?"

"I don't know."

Like a broken record, this one.

"It's—it's been a long couple of days."

Her eyes started to water, and she rubbed them with the back of her ungloved hands. She might be lying about how she came to be here, but those tears were real.

As sheriff—hell, as a decent human being—he couldn't ignore her plight.

Swinging his leg over the saddle, Ryder hopped down from Wind Chaser. He kept the reins in his hand as he stepped closer. "It's okay. Don't worry about it. I can take you into town, and we'll find your car later."

She glanced up, and for the first time, he noticed her eyes. Not blue, not green, but a mix of both, with little gold flecks speckled around the irises. The most beautiful eyes he'd ever seen.

Damn. Her gaze sucker punched him right in the gut.

"Uh, we don't have a hospital in town." He stumbled over his words, trying to regain his wits. "But there's a local doc I can call if you—"

"I don't need a doctor," she said quickly.

"You sure? People can't always tell if they're hurt

after an accident. Adrenalin can mask pain."

She let out a dry laugh. "Oh, I can feel plenty of pain. My feet are so cold it feels like I'm walking on shards of glass."

He glanced down and grimaced. "For future reference, heels are not the best footwear for trudging through snow."

Those amazing eyes narrowed. "I wasn't *planning* on doing any snow trudging."

"Right." He let his gaze roam over her as he speculated. "You just got stuck out here because your car broke down, and tromping through the woods seemed like the way to solve the problem."

"Something like that," she grumbled through her teeth.

Ryder shook his head. Usually, he was great with people, women especially. He was a nice, friendly guy. His pleasant demeanor helped him nab the bad guy more than a time or two. He always played good cop. So, why was he baiting this woman? Maybe he was cranky from the cold.

The cold.

Shit, I am an ass.

Here he was trying to get the truth out of whoever this lady was, and she could very well be catching hypothermia as they spoke.

Stellar police work there, Ryder.

"Come on." He took her arm gently.

She pulled away with a sharp intake of breath.

He paused at the expression on her face, one of pure terror. *What the hell happened to her?*

Hands up in a nonthreatening manner, he said, "Easy now. I was just going to put you on Wind Chaser and ride you into town."

Those fearful, hazel eyes darted back and forth between horse and man.

"We only have one hotel. Its doors close at nine, but I can call up Roger and see if he has a room for you."

A million emotions passed over her expressive face, but Ryder focused on the one most prominent.

Desperation.

He'd bet the farm she was running from something. What, he wasn't sure.

"If you'd prefer," he said, speaking before he even thought it through, "you can stay with me for the night."

That got her attention. Her breath came faster, and she glanced around for escape routes. Damn, he hadn't meant to scare her. To make it sound like *that*.

"I have an extra room," he explained, trying to clear up the miscommunication. "There's a lock on the door and everything. I know you don't know me from Adam, but I swear, I'm not some kind of pervert or serial killer. I'm just trying to help."

She worried her bottom lip, indecision plain on her face, her voice soft as she asked, "Why?"

He felt a sad smile kick up the corner of his mouth. What happened to this poor woman to make her so skeptical?

"Because you look like you need it."

A sob broke from her lip, but she swallowed it back down and blinked the tears away.

Terrified, wary, but strong. Damn, she was something.

She nodded slowly, then with more vigor. "Okay.

I'll stay with you."

His smile was genuine this time. "Great. Ever ride a horse before?"

Her eyes went wide, and she shook her head.

He laughed. "Nothing to worry about. It's just like riding a bike. Except you don't have to pedal."

"A bike on steroids maybe," she muttered.

Not wanting to spook her again, Ryder held out his hand this time instead of grabbing her arm. Reluctantly, she placed hers in his.

"Jesus, you're freezing."

"I passed freezing half an hour ago."

Bringing her to Wind Chaser's side, he showed her how to place a foot in the stirrup. She gripped the saddle horn and swung her leg over. Her momentum didn't quite make it. As she started to fall back, he placed his hand on her backside and hoisted her up onto the saddle.

"Thanks," she mumbled, sitting stock still.

"Yeah. No problem."

Ryder untied the riding blanket strapped onto the back of his saddle and tried not to think about how lush and warm her sweet, round cheeks had felt in his hands.

Get it together, man.

The woman was half-frozen and terrified to boot. She didn't need him lusting after her like a horny schoolboy just because he accidently copped a feel. No matter how amazing the feel had been.

Hoisting himself up behind her, he unrolled the blanket and wrapped it around her.

"Here, this will help keep you warm until we get back to my place."

She accepted with a grateful nod, burrowing into it.

He nudged Wind Chaser, and the horse set off for home. The woman, whose name he still hadn't gotten, held herself stiff in the saddle against him. Soon, however, the rocking motion of the horse's steps lulled her into relaxation.

Ryder wrapped an arm around her as he realized she'd fallen asleep, head falling back against him, her cold-reddened cheek resting against his chest. Tucking her close to his body, he gazed down at her face, taking a good look at it for the first time. Small, round, with high, delicate cheekbones, a slim nose, and the most lush, kissable lips he had ever seen...

What the hell is wrong with me? This woman was obviously in some kind of trouble, and here he was wondering if she tasted as good as she looked.

Wandering the woods in the middle of the night, in clothing more suited to a mall outing than a winter hike, she was hiding something and lying to him with every word that came out of her pretty little mouth. As an officer of the law, truth was of the utmost importance to him. She should *not* fascinate him.

So, why was he taking her to his home instead of the hotel, or station? Why was he holding her in his arms as if she were precious? And why did it feel so right to have her there?

Chapter 3

A delicious smell woke her—the smell of bacon frying. Strange, Jen was a vegetarian. Kayla loved the stuff, but out of respect for her friend, she never cooked it at home.

Why would Jen be cooking bacon?

Her eyes fluttered open. As she took in the strange surroundings, the past few days came crashing back. Jen wasn't cooking bacon—Jen was dead. And Kayla wasn't at home. She was...

She had no idea, really. All she knew was the man last night, Ryder, found her in the woods and offered her a ride back to his house. So, here she was in a strange man's home.

Am I crazy? This is how all those serial killer movies start.

It had seemed like a good idea at the time. Better than freezing to death in the woods or risking another creepy trucker ride. She'd take a bedroom door with a lock over a truck cab any day.

Kayla still couldn't believe she rode an actual horse last night. The thing had been huge. Horses never looked that big on TV.

Had she fallen asleep? She must have, because she didn't remember arriving at Ryder's home. Yet, here she was, snuggled into the warmest, comfiest bed she had ever been in. She glanced around the room, about the same size as hers back home. The queen-sized bed took up a good portion of the space, and there was a small closet along the far wall and a large oak dresser near the window.

A picture of Ryder hugging an attractive looking woman in a cap and gown, with similar features and identical long, dark hair, sat on top of the dresser. They both looked so happy. Judging by the likeness, she guessed them to be siblings.

Her heart clutched again, the image reminded her of Jen, her sister at heart. It was so unfair what had happened to her.

I can't let David get away with it.

But how would she be able to prove what a monster he was if she had to keep running and hiding?

Her stomach growled, reminding her it had been almost a day since she had eaten. The chips she scarfed down from the bus stop vending machine yesterday morning were the last things she remembered eating.

Dang, the bacon smell was really getting to her.

Tossing aside the warm comforter, she rose from the bed. She looked down, noticing she still wore her clothing from yesterday. Her coat and shoes had been removed. By her or Ryder? Since she didn't remember disrobing and hopping into this very comfortable bed, it must have been him. He left her clothes on; that gave credence to him being a good guy, right?

The hardwood floor pricked like ice under her bare feet. Kayla walked to the closet on tiptoes, to minimize her exposure to the chilly floor. Hopefully, there would be some slippers or warm socks in there for her to borrow.

Bingo!

There on the floor, she spotted a pair of brown, furry, boot-like slippers. She also grabbed a blue knit sweater from a coat hanger. Pulling it over her head, she left the bedroom in search of the delicious smelling bacon. It didn't take her long to find. A quick walk down the hall and she found herself in a bright, cheery-looking kitchen.

Sunlight poured in from a bay window, where a small, round table with two chairs sat. White cabinets with blue trim gave the kitchen a country farm feel. Stainless steel appliances kept the room from looking too old fashion. And there, cooking at the stove, with his back to her, stood Ryder.

Delicious smells of bacon, eggs, and coffee wafted in the air between them. Her tummy gave a soft rumble of anticipation.

"Oh good, you're up."

The man had ears like a bat.

"I was just about to come and wake you. Breakfast is all ready." He glanced over his shoulder, gave her a smile, and motioned with his head toward the small table. "Have a seat."

Kayla walked over and sat. A quick glance around the kitchen revealed nothing unusual. Appliances, dishes, an aloe plant by the window. No severed heads or chains bolted to the wall. So, highly unlikely Ryder was a psycho killer.

She scoffed to herself. *Yeah, like the guy would keep that stuff out in plain sight.*

Still, if he'd wanted to hurt her, he could have done it last night when she fell into exhausted unconsciousness.

Unless he's lulling me into a false sense of

security.

It didn't feel like that to her, but she'd be smart to keep her wits. David was a stark reminder of how wrong she could be about a person.

"Here's some coffee to start you out." Ryder brought a steaming hot cup over to her. "Cream and sugar?"

She nodded, and he smiled again, turning from her to retrieve the items from the counter.

Good gravy, the man's handsome.

She had been sure her impression of him last night was a side effect of sleep deprivation. No such luck. Jake Ryder was even better looking this morning than he had been last night. In the light of the day, she could see much better. Smooth, tanned skin and sharp features, which should have made him hard, only served to increase his appeal. His smile was as devastating as those rich, chocolate eyes.

And don't even get her started on that hair. It hung down his back, loose and beautiful. Normally, she didn't like long hair on men, but on Ryder, somehow, it fit. It was so sleek and shiny. Her fingers ached to touch it. She wanted to run her hands through those silky stands and see if they were as soft as they looked.

What the heck is wrong with me?

She was on the run. Wanted for trumped up murder charges, and here she was mooning over her late night rescuer. Fine time for her libido to kick in.

Blame it on all the adrenalin.

"Here you go." He placed a plate of piping hot food in front of her. "I hope you like scrambled. Every time I try to do over-easy, I end up popping the yolk."

He lifted his shoulders in a sheepish shrug she

found adorable.

No, no she did not. She found it nothing. He was not adorable or sexy or anything.

Focus, Kayla. Running for your life, not looking for a date to the prom.

She glanced at him again and frowned. Good looking, seemingly normal, who else did that describe? David Tyler. Look how well her assumption of him turned out.

The devil hides behind an angel's face.

Wasn't that the phrase? She'd do well to remember this man, though generous and good-natured now, could turn on a dime. Could you ever really know someone?

"So." He took the seat across from her, his own plate in hand. "How do you feel this morning?"

"Fine." She took a bite of her eggs—*oh man, even better than they smell*—and shrugged.

He took a sip of his coffee, watching her over the rim of the mug. She shifted in her seat under his scrutiny, letting her gaze drift to the window. Snow, trees, and more snow.

"Where am I?"

His brow drew down. "My house. You agreed to come here last night, remember?"

"No, I mean, *where* is your house?"

Circumspection entered his gaze as he answered, "Peak Town. Colorado."

Colorado? She'd traveled far. Hopefully, far enough to escape David and the Chicago PD.

"You know, I never did catch your name last night."

Suspicion colored his voice. What could she tell

him? Had they received word about Kayla Jenkins, wanted fugitive, all the way out here in Peak Town, Colorado? Should she use a false name? Something more common, like Jane Smith?

Oh yeah, 'cause that's not suspicious at all.

"I, um…can't remember."

"You can't remember?" Disbelief dripped off every word.

"I hit my head when my car ran off the road. Memory is still a little fuzzy." There, that should do it. People got amnesia from head trauma all the time. She could sell this.

"Kayla."

"What?"

"Your name is Kayla."

Fear shot through her like a red-hot poker. He knew her name. The news *had* spread to Peak Town. Maybe there was a reward, and Ryder had been toying with her. He was just waiting to call the cops, call David. She would be thrown in jail, and no one would ever know what really happened to Jen.

"It's on your necklace." One long finger pointed to her chest.

Her hand fluttered to the gold chain hanging from her neck. A Christmas present from Jen three years ago. She probably should have ditched the jewelry along with her identification back in Kansas, but she couldn't bear to part with it. The sentimental gift was now the only thing she had left of her friend.

"I figure if you wear a piece of jewelry with a name on it, must be yours, right?"

She shrugged, neither confirming nor denying.

"Mmm hmm."

They ate in silence. Once Ryder cleared his plate, he went to the pot and refilled his coffee. He offered more to her, but she declined.

"Shame about your memory. You sure you don't want to see the doc?"

She shook her head.

"Head injuries can be tricky, especially with memory loss."

The skepticism in his voice had her cursing her poor bluffing skills. "I'm fine."

He shrugged. "Still, can't let you go about not knowing who you are."

Oh yes he could. The less he knew about her, the better.

"Not a problem, though. I can help you find your identity."

Shoot! Just what she needed, a nosy Dudley-Do-Right trying to help her.

"That's not necessary. Thank you for your help last night and breakfast this morning, but I really should get going."

"And where are you going to go with no car and no memory?"

Funny thing was, she actually had no idea, but she knew staying here was not an option. "I'll figure it out."

"I can help."

"What makes you think so?"

He toyed with the rim of his coffee mug, expression unreadable. "I have resources."

Resources? What kind of identity finding resources could a cowboy have?

"Like what?"

He took a sip of his coffee, those penetrating eyes

focused on her. "Records."

"Records?" *Like music?*

He nodded. "DMV, arrest, background checks."

The fork froze on the way to her mouth, blood turning to ice in her veins. *Oh no, please, please no—"* You a P.I. or something?" *Please be or something.*

"Nope." Ryder shook his head, taking another sip of coffee before continuing. "I'm the sheriff here in Peak Town."

Her vision dimmed. Blinding terror blazed through her. Not another cop. He would never believe her. If he knew who she really was, he'd send her straight to the Chicago PD...and David. He could find out, too. So easy. Just one fingerprint—as a schoolteacher, hers were on record.

She had to get out, now.

In her haste to stand, she knocked against the table, causing her coffee cup to tip over onto the floor. She shrieked as the shattered ceramic pieces scattered along the hardwood.

Ryder was there in an instant, pulling her to him, wrapping his arms around her in comfort. "Hey, hey, hey. It's all right. Just a broken mug. No reason to panic."

She froze against him as her body warred with her mind.

He smells so good.

He's a cop.

His arms are so strong and soothing.

He'll arrest me in a heartbeat if he knew who I am.

At least he isn't a psycho killer.

"You okay?"

She had to play along. Not act like a crazy woman.

21

That would raise his suspicions even more. She had to keep up the amnesiac pretense until she could sneak away. Because she *was* sure of one thing, as an officer of the law, Ryder would never let her go until he had answers. So, she had to keep it together for a little while longer. Until she found a chance to run.

"Yes, I'm fine. Just a little on edge from everything I guess." Kayla pulled out of his embrace. "It would be great if you could help me find my identity. Thank you." She pasted on what she hoped was a convincing smile.

He looked down at her, the skepticism plain on his face. "Not a problem. We can head down to the station later today—"

"*No.*"

He raised a brow at her sharp denial.

She smiled again, trying to cover her outburst. "I mean, I'm still really tired and sore from the accident. I would really like to take it easy today. Maybe soak in a warm tub? I think my feet are still a bit frozen." She tried for a laugh, but it fell flat.

"Sure," he said, staring intently at her. "I have the day off today anyway. I guess I can take you in tomorrow, and we can run a fingerprint scan. See if you're in the system."

Her teeth clenched together as she tried to hold the smile. "Great."

Not great. So not great.

Heart pounding in her chest, she tried to effect an air of calm. Hard to do when terror made every limb tremble. Could he hear her uneven breathing? *Gees*, she sounded like a Lamaze patient.

But, once he fingerprinted her, it would all be over.

Her wanted poster would come up, and Ryder would hand her in. Just like David wanted. No matter what she said, no one would believe her. She would go to prison for Jen's murder, and David would forever play the grieving boyfriend.

She couldn't let that happen. Ryder could not discover who she was. She had to run, as soon as possible.

Chapter 4

Amnesia my ass.

Kayla was a terrible liar. Even if he hadn't been good at spotting frauds—a handy skill he picked up in the police academy—Ryder would have seen through this woman's fabrications.

Her story sounded like the plot of one of those daytime TV soaps his mother enjoyed. Memory problems were always convenient. No, Kayla was running from something, that much was clear. Something…or someone.

Poor woman damn near jumped out of her skin when he mentioned he was the sheriff. So, she had a problem with law enforcement? She didn't look like a criminal. Then again, in the decade or so he'd been on the force, he learned looks could be deceiving. No one had ever suspected the actual culprit who sabotaged Maggie's cupcake shop. A pretty face could often hide deceitful acts. And Kayla had one of the prettiest faces he'd ever seen.

Shit. He had to stop thinking along those lines. This woman could be a bank robber for all he knew. He couldn't think with his little head. Not until he knew who she was and why she was so wary of…everything.

She *was* afraid, that much he could see. Of being caught? No matter how hard he tried, Ryder couldn't see this woman as a criminal. Maybe he was thinking with his dick, but she didn't give off the bad guy vibe. Didn't mean he wasn't going to check her out. He had a duty to protect the people of his town.

Kayla gathered the breakfast dishes, bringing them to the sink.

"Don't worry about those," he said as she started to fill the sink with soapy water. "I'll take care of them."

She sent him a small smile, a genuine one, nearly knocking him on his ass. Damn, the woman truly was beautiful.

"You rescued me last night, gave me a warm place to sleep, and cooked me breakfast this morning. The least I can do is wash the dishes."

She looked determined, so he didn't argue. Instead, he asked, "Want me to run you a hot bath?"

A small moan escaped her lips. Every nerve ending in his body sat up and took notice at the sensual sound. The semi-hard he'd been sporting since he saw her this morning turned into a full-blown erection, straining against his zipper as he imagined her making those soft, sweet, noises while he thrust into her.

Dammit. The image was so vivid he could taste it.

Ryder cleared his throat. "I'll take that as a yes?"

"I would love a hot bath." She didn't turn as she spoke, still scrubbing away at the dishes.

"Just come down the hall when you're done. First door on the left."

He turned then, before he did something embarrassing like pull her into his arms and see if he could get her to make more of those boner-inspiring moans.

What is wrong with me?

His reaction to this woman was strange. He wasn't

sure he liked it. He knew nothing about her—except she was lying to him—and yet he still wanted her. And not just in a sexual way. There was something about Kayla that made him want to protect her, care for her. Something deep inside told him this woman was connected to him on a level he couldn't fathom.

The thought was scary as hell.

Without another word, he headed down the hallway to the bathroom. He twisted the taps, waited until the temp was hot but not scalding, and filled the tub. Glancing around, he spotted some lavender bubble bath his sister had left last time she visited.

Women liked bubble baths, right?

His sister sure did, so he figured Kayla would enjoy them, too.

He poured the floral-scented gel into the bath, watching as the running water turned it into white, foamy bubbles filling the round tub.

Why am I doing this?

He should be interrogating this woman in town. Not pampering her with breakfast and bubble baths.

"Oh, wow."

The soft exclamation came from behind him. He turned and saw the mysterious woman currently turning his brain to mush.

"Perfect timing." He turned off the faucet as the tub finished filling. "It's all ready."

"You drew me a bubble bath?"

Her brow drew down in confusion. At his consideration, or the fact that he, a man, had bubble bath?

"Yeah." Ryder rubbed the back of his neck, embarrassed now by his overt efforts. "My, uh, sister likes bubble baths. So I figured..."

"Thank you," she said with a small grin. "That's very sweet of you."

Sweet? No one but his mother had ever called him sweet before. Nice, sure. Fun and charming had been whispered by a few ladies, but sweet? No one thought of a sheriff as sweet.

"Well, enjoy." He made a hasty exit from the room.

While Kayla was occupied in her bath, he planned to do what he should have done from the start. Try to discover who she was.

Making his way to the small office at the back of the house, Ryder booted up his computer and connected to the station's system. Peak Town may be a small mountain community, but they still had twenty-first century technology. He logged in and ran a missing person search using Kayla's description and first name.

Female, mid-twenties—he was guessing on that—approximately five-five, one hundred and thirty—again guessing—short brown hair that looked like someone had taken a weed whacker to it, hazel eyes. Amazing, hazel eyes that turned his brain into Silly Putty.

There was no box for the last description.

After a few minutes, the computer dinged with the results. Ryder scowled.

Zero. No Matches Found.

Not a missing person. Looked like he was going to have to interrogate Kayla after all.

****

He made me a bubble bath.

Kayla soaked in the warm, sweet smelling water. She didn't understand Ryder. He didn't buy her "I can't remember" story. No big surprise there—she had never been a very good liar, and the man was obviously no idiot. But, if he knew she was lying, why didn't he call her on it? Haul her downtown and lock her up 'til she talked? He could do it.

Sheriff, ugh!

Running from one cop right smack into another. *How about that for crappy luck?*

At least this one wasn't trying to frame her for murder. Though, the second he discovered her real identity, he might turn her over to the one who was.

She shouldn't be soaking in his tub; she needed to make her escape. But her limbs were finally warm. No reason she couldn't bathe *and* plan, right?

A shame, really. Another time, different circumstances, she would have loved to stay. Jake Ryder was one sexy sheriff. Kind, too. As evidenced by breakfast and the bubble bath currently pruning her body. If only they could have met in a bar or at a mutual friend's party. Only, that never would have happened. They lived states away. Highly unlikely they would have met if she hadn't been on the run.

Something deep inside whispered a denial.

Kayla had never been very religious. Hard to follow specific church teachings when you went to a different church every year. A lot of her foster families were Christian, but the denominations always changed. Catholic, Protestant, Baptist. She even stayed with a Universal Unitarian once. Foster kids quickly learned to believe whatever the person who fed you at the moment told you. Otherwise, you might not get fed.

Once she was on her own, she stopped going to church. She did believe in some kind of higher power;

she just wasn't sure what it was. God, the Universe, Space Aliens. Okay, probably not aliens. Whatever was out there, did it lead her to this man?

Too bad she couldn't stick around to find out. She had to keep moving. There was no other option. Maybe, if she was lucky, the universe would put her and Ryder together again. When they weren't on opposite sides of the law.

A soft knock pulled her from her thoughts.

"You doing okay in there?" Ryder's deep voice carried through the solid oak door.

"Yup. I'm just about done." Only then did she realize the water had cooled. How long had she sat in here musing?

"I left some clothes for you right outside the door."

There he went again with the thoughtfulness. "Thanks."

"Come into the living room when you're dressed, and we'll talk some more."

Talk, yeah right. She'd heard the shift in his tone. Thoughtful Ryder had been replaced with Sheriff Ryder. The man flew back and forth between the two so fast it gave her whiplash.

Kayla pulled the rubber tub stopper. Cold, sudsy water swirled down the drain. She rose, grabbing one of the soft, terry cloth towels hanging from the wall rack. Drying quickly, she stepped out of the tub. Making sure the towel was secured tightly around her, she opened the door a crack and peeked out. The hallway was empty, but as promised, a pile of clothing lay on the ground in front of the bathroom door.

She grabbed it and quickly shut the door again. A pair of woman's jeans, a light blue T-shirt and a beautiful gray, cashmere sweater.

Why did Ryder have women's clothing so readily available? Was he married? Dating someone? Ten minutes ago, she had been pondering the strange connection she felt to this man…and she hadn't even questioned if he was single. This running for her life thing was really messing with her head.

She removed her towel and started to dress. He'd provided no underwear or bra, but that was just as well. Borrowing clothes was one thing. Borrowing undergarments? *Ew! No thank you.* She'd go commando.

Kayla went to wrap her hair in the towel, then remembered she no longer had long locks which required the standard female turban towel wrap. Least of her issues at the moment, but still, feminine vanity tightened her chest; she missed her long hair. A quick rub of the towel on her head and her short, dyed hair was almost dry. Guess that made one positive thing about this whole situation. Normally, her hair took hours to dry if she didn't blow it out.

The bathroom door creaked as she opened it. "Ryder?"

"In the living room," he called.

Right, he'd told her that's where he would be. Toeing on the borrowed slippers from this morning, she made her way down the hall. A crackling fire roared in the fireplace. It smelled homey and gave the room a toasty, warm feel.

"Looks like everything fit okay."

Ryder gave her a smile, making her knees go a little weak. "Yes, thank you." She cleared her throat and tried for casual. "Do these clothes belong to your wife?"

His grin widened. "Not married."

"Girlfriend?" she tried again.

Chocolate brown eyes danced with mischief. "Nope."

Was he being obtuse on purpose? Her brow furrowed as she thought of other possibilities of the readily available women's clothing. No wife, no girlfriend. Did he have a string of women parading around his house? So many that he had to keep spare clothing on hand?

He chuckled at her pathetic attempts of subtlety. "They're my sister's. Julie lives in Aspen, but comes to stay with me from time to time. She leaves a few spare changes of clothes in the guest room in case she ever stays the night unexpectedly."

Right, the closet where she got the slippers and sweater this morning. Her mind drifted back to the picture on the dresser, the one of Ryder standing with his arm around a woman who looked like him. His sister; she'd been right.

"I hope she doesn't mind."

He waved a hand in the air. "Naw. Julie's always willing to help out a person in need. It's kind of what she does for a living."

"Oh?"

"Yeah. She's a lawyer."

Lawyer? A sheriff *and* a lawyer, all in one family. *Great.* Ryder could arrest her, and his sister could prosecute. This running away thing was going swimmingly—too bad she never learned to swim.

"I wanted to talk a little more about your memory problems."

Here it comes. She swallowed past the lump of fear clogging her throat.

"I did a missing persons search."

Oh shoot!

Her pulse skyrocketed. Biting the inside of her cheek to keep from hyperventilating, she waited.

"I figured someone might be looking for you."

Yeah. The entire Chicago PD.

"Came up empty. No Kaylas matching your description missing in the area."

She faked a yawn, covering her sigh of relief. Technically, she wasn't a missing person. She was a *wanted* person. And she had changed her "description" because of her wanted status. The information on her must not have left Illinois yet. She prayed it stayed that way until she had a chance to sneak away.

"We'll go to the station tomorrow and run your prints." Ryder stared intently at her. His gaze compelled her to spill her secrets.

No such luck, buddy. Amnesia. That was her story, and she was sticking to it.

"They should turn up something."

"Sounds good." No it didn't. Sounded like her doom. Which was why she would not be here tomorrow. "I think I'll go lay down for a bit. I'm still pretty tired."

He nodded, but she could see his intelligent cop brain working behind those bedroom eyes. It really was too bad they had to meet like this. Her last relationship ended six months ago, and three days ago she'd decided she was ready to end her dry spell. Ryder would've been the perfect man to end it with. But now, she was on the run from the cops, which he just so happened to be. Perhaps in another life they could have gotten together, had some fun, maybe even developed something lasting.

Longing ached in her chest. She tucked her hands behind her back to keep from reaching out for some physical comfort, human connection. A hopeless sigh escaped her as she turned to leave. Right now, she had to focus on this life, because if she wasn't careful. She might not have it for long.

Chapter 5

The sun had sunk behind the western mountains when the sounds of Kayla moving about came from his guest room. Whether she had been sleeping or avoiding him, he didn't know.

He'd tried his search again. Widening the parameters, but still came up empty. If she was missing, no one had reported her as such.

A sad situation, in his opinion.

Ryder knew if *he* didn't show up for work people would start asking for his whereabouts. And not just because he was the sheriff. His sister would call in the National Guard if he missed a call from her and failed to return it after a reasonable amount of time.

When their mother died, Julie had taken it upon herself to make sure he was eating right, getting enough sleep, and in general good health. Her mothering struck him as funny, because she was four years his junior. He had been the one who stepped up after their dad died, became the man of the house as much as he could. Got a job, fixed things that needed tending to, threatened any boy who got within six inches of his sweet, innocent, baby sister. Now, Julie had turned the tables and taken on the parental roll. He knew how much she missed their mother, so he let it slide for the most part. It made him sad to think Kayla had no one who cared for her enough to report her missing.

"Something sure smells good."

I think of her, and she arrives.

"Looks like I slept through lunch." She gave him a sheepish smile, wrinkling her nose. "Sorry. Guess I was more tired than I thought."

She looked like she just got out of bed—clothes rumpled, hair mussed. It conjured up images of her in his bed. He'd like to peel the wrinkled clothing from her, muss her hair up even more as he sank into her sweet, warm body. Drive her wild with pleasure. Maybe even hear a few sexy, little moans as she came apart in his arms.

Oh, yeah. There's an image he liked. A little too much, judging by the tightening in his pants.

He turned back to the stove and stirred the stew, mentally telling his raging libido to behave. "Don't worry about it. You needed to recover."

"So…um, what did you do all day while I slept?"

A glance over his shoulder revealed Kayla's gaze darting about the place.

Looking for something, sweetheart? Wondering if I've been checking into you?

Not that it had done him any good. Focusing his own gaze on the task at hand, he answered, "Tended to Wind Chaser, did a little reading."

A sigh of relief sounded behind him, and he wondered if she would still be relieved if she knew his reading consisted of Internet searches for a missing woman named Kayla.

Probably not.

"What's that?" she asked, coming to stand beside him.

His entire body tensed with anticipation when her

arm brushed against his. He never reacted this way to a woman before. There had been women he lusted after, cared about, one he even thought he loved, but none of them hit him on such a primal level. This was crazy. He didn't even know this woman.

"It's cowboy stew. My dad's recipe."

"Smells amazing. Can I help with anything?"

She could help with the rapidly rising problem in his jeans.

"Sure. You can set the table. Bowls are in that cupboard." He pointed to the cabinet beside the sink. "Spoons in the drawer below."

Kayla moved off to gather the dishes, and he let out a sigh of reprieve. How was he going to discover who this woman was when every time he got close to her he wanted to rip off her clothes and take her on the nearest flat surface? Or round surface. Up against the wall…hell, he didn't care. He just wanted her.

Obviously, it had been too long since he got laid if a potential criminal got him all hot and bothered.

"Drinks?"

"Milk and iced tea in the fridge," he replied. "Beer, too. Sorry, I don't have any wine or anything." His sister always brought wine when she came up. Said beer tasted bitter. Never tasted bitter to him.

"I'll just have some tea, thanks." She opened the fridge and grabbed the pitcher. "You want a beer?"

Normally, he'd say yes, but he needed to keep his wits about him with Kayla around. For one thing, he wanted to uncover some answers. Then there was the other reason, the one where he wanted her with an unexplainable desire. Hard enough keeping his hands to himself sober; booze would make it impossible.

"Tea is fine."

She passed by with the iced tea pitcher in hand. His kitchen was on the small side, and he took up a lot of space. When she moved around him, her shoulder grazed his back. He stifled a groan. One small touch, from her shoulder no less, and his body burned with hunger.

Good call on skipping the booze. Things were already *hard enough* as it was.

"Stew's on." He brought the steaming pot over to the table. Setting it on the potholder he laid out earlier, he grabbed the bowls and filled them. "Hope you like it."

She took a bite. Her eyes closed and another one of those sexy moans escaped. Good lord, this woman would be the death of him.

"Oh. My. Goodness. This is amazing." She smiled.

"Glad you like it."

"No, seriously. I want to call up your dad right now and thank him for creating this recipe, it's that good."

"I'm sure he'd be happy to hear that, but unfortunately, he passed." The dull ache he got in his chest whenever he thought of his father caused him to glance down at the dinner. No matter how much time passed, it always hurt, but remembering the good things—like his dad making stew—made him smile.

Her spoon paused on the way to her mouth, smile faltering. "Oh, Ryder. I'm sorry."

He shifted in his seat. "It's all right. It was a long time ago."

"How old were you when he died?"

"Sixteen." He pushed his stew around in the bowl, watching the potatoes and corn circle each other, but

37

seeing his dad's face in his mind. "He died two weeks before my seventeenth birthday."

"How awful."

Yeah, it had been. His dad had been talking all month long about Ryder's "special day." The old man had something really big planned. Later, his mother told him it had been a trip to Maine to hike the Appalachian Trail. Something the two had been talking about for years, but his father said he needed to be old enough to handle it. It was supposed to be his rite of passage, his journey into manhood...

Instead, some jackass had plowed head first into his dad's car. He *had* become a man that day...by necessity.

"What happened? If you don't mind me asking." Her words were soft, spoken with empathy, not pity.

"I don't mind." He shook his head. Most people were curious about death, human nature he guessed, but she sounded genuinely concerned. Still, it wasn't easy to talk about. Pushing his dinner around, he spoke quickly, as if speed would keep the pain at bay. "He got hit by a drunk driver on the way home from work. Guy blew a one point nine. Walked away without a scratch. EMT said my dad died on impact."

"That's so unfair."

He looked up and saw tears shining in her eyes. Tears for him, for his family, from a woman he barely knew.

"Yeah." He learned that day life was rarely fair. "The guy got fifteen years for vehicular homicide."

"Doesn't seem long enough to me."

He agreed. "The driver had four previous DUIs. He shouldn't have even had a license." His grip tightened on his spoon.

"For heaven's sake, why did he?"

Ryder shrugged, but the motion belied the anger he still felt. "Slipped through the cracks I guess."

Her gaze softened and the corner of her lips turned up in small smile. "Is that why you went into law enforcement? To make sure the bad guys are kept off the streets?"

He nodded. "Yeah. My father's death was a turning point in my life. It was the reason my sister decided to get into law, too. She's a prosecutor. Mom always said I catch 'em and Julie makes sure to lock 'em up."

Kayla's smile tightened at that, but she quickly covered it with another question. "And where's your mom now?"

"She passed away three years ago. Cancer." He shoveled a spoonful of food into his mouth, as if stuffing his face could fill the hole in his heart. It started with his father and only grew bigger when his mother passed.

A stricken look passed over her face. Her hand grasped his tightly, and she squeezed. "I'm sorry. To lose both your parents? That's hard. I'm sorry I brought it up."

He enjoyed the feel of her soft, delicate hand in his large, rough one. "I'm sorry I keep bringing the dinner conversation down with my tales of family loss." He stroked the back of her hand with the pad of his thumb. "I hope I didn't spoil your appetite."

She gave him a sad smile. "You didn't spoil anything. But if you'd like to switch to a happier topic, I'm okay with that."

Yes please. Talking about his parents' passing was

not his favorite subject.

He laughed. "You got it."

She released his hand, and he immediately felt the loss. This woman was really twisting him in knots.

"A happier topic, huh? Well, since you can't tell me about your family…"

She shrugged, suddenly very interested in her soup.

That's right, sweetheart. Keep up your silly, forgetful game. I'll uncover your secrets soon enough. He always did.

"Guess we'll have to discuss the warm, balmy weather outside and which pumps go best with snow banks."

She laughed, as he intended.

They spent the rest of dinner discussing trivial things like weather, sports, and television shows. He didn't call her on the fact she could remember her favorite late night talk show host, but couldn't remember her name. Every bit of information he gleaned from her, he stored away for future dissection. She would slip up at some point. Everyone did.

After the way she'd sympathized over his parents, he felt a little guilty about being so sneaky. He could feel her heartbreak for him. Humbling for a stranger to show so much compassion. Made him feel like an ass for digging into her past without her realizing it. But, since she refused to tell him anything, he had to start somewhere.

Over the course of the meal, she revealed she loved Fallon over Letterman and the Bears over the Packers. The former gave him nothing, but the latter proved interesting. He wasn't a huge sports fan, but even he knew of the Bears versus Packers rivalry. Her fervor for the Bears pointed to her having a connection to Illinois. Most likely Chicago or nearby. By the end of dinner, he felt he had a solid lead to go on.

Kayla insisted on doing the dishes again. He agreed, only so long as he helped.

They washed and dried in perfect sync. It was strange. Almost like they had been performing this task for years. He really needed to discover who this woman was before things got out of hand.

"Thank you, Ryder." She dried her hands on a kitchen towel. "For everything."

He narrowed his eyes. Now, why did that sound like a goodbye?

"You're a good man. I'm sure your parents would have been proud." Stretching up on her toes, she placed a soft, too brief kiss right smack on his lips. Then she walked away.

Not until he heard the bedroom door close did he realize what just happened. Kayla had kissed him, and not a "thank you" kiss—that was a goodbye kiss.

Son of a bitch.

She was planning on sneaking out in the middle of the night. He would bet the farm on it, if he had a farm.

Well, that wasn't going to happen. He wasn't finished with Ms. "I Have Amnesia" Kayla. Not by a long shot. If she thought she could give him the slip, she had another thing coming.

Shutting off the lights, Ryder went to the living room and sat in the dark. He'd done a stake out or two in his day. Waiting for Kayla to sneak away would be no sweat. He'd tried asking her, coaxing her, even tried a little trickery. Good cop wasn't working.

He'd wait, sure it wouldn't be long.

A smile curved his lips as he remembered her soft kiss. It had been a goodbye, true, but there had also been desire behind it. He saw it in those incredible hazel eyes. Felt it in the rapid beat of her pulse. She felt this strange attraction, same as him. He could use that to his advantage.

Good cop wasn't working? Fine. He grinned with anticipation. Then he'd have to bring out bad cop.

And he could be very, very bad.

Chapter 6

The clock on the dresser displayed a red glowing twelve. Midnight. Five hours had passed since she shut herself away in the guest room.

Ryder should be asleep by now.

Kayla threw off the covers. Guilt prickled as she grabbed the bag she'd stashed under the bed. Normally, she would never take something that didn't belong to her, but these were extenuating circumstances. When she saw the brown leather backpack in the closet while replacing the slippers earlier, she didn't hesitate. She couldn't keep running in dirty slacks, a T-shirt, and her pumps.

So, she'd taken advantage of Ryder—and by extension, his sister's—kindness and filled the bag with a few spare shirts, two pairs of jeans, and half a dozen socks. She also borrowed a pair of boots. Julie Ryder's feet were a smidge smaller than hers, but cramped warm feet beat out frozen ones any day.

Her coat hung on a rack by the door. She'd seen it earlier at dinner.

Thinking of dinner reminded her of Ryder's candid confession about the death of his parents. Her heart broke for him when he spoke of them. Having never known hers, she always imagined what it would be like to have a loving mother and father. Every Christmas as a child, she asked Santa for parents to love and protect her. It seemed so unfair for everyone else to have them. Why not her?

After hearing about Ryder's father, though, she wondered if she was better off. To have a father who loved you and then lose him to such a horrible tragedy must have been awful. Then to lose your mother to such a terrible disease, it seemed almost too cruel. Maybe she'd been better off not knowing her parents. With no family, she'd had no one to lose.

Except Jen.

Tears burned her eyes, and she let them fall. A sob threatened to break free, but she choked it back—she couldn't risk waking Ryder. But flashes of Jen's lifeless body kept playing in her memory like a macabre horror movie.

Blood, so much blood everywhere.

She closed her eyes, but that made the images sharpen in her mind. Tremors racked her body, shaking her so hard her teeth rattled. Wrapping her arms around herself, she breathed in deep, pushing for control. No time to fall apart now; she had to press on. Dealing with the loss of her best friend would have to wait.

When Ryder bared his family tragedy at dinner, she wanted to do more. Take him in her arms. Comfort him. Ease his pain, because the pain was still there. She saw it in those expressive, deep brown eyes. But she hadn't done any of those things. If she had done more than touch his hand, she knew she would have been lost. Jen had been her family. Now, she was gone, and Kayla felt as if a piece of her was missing, something she could never replace or find again. Yes, she would definitely say losing someone you loved hurt worse than wishing for someone you never knew.

It had taken all her willpower to keep her goodbye kiss light and soft when what she really wanted to do was toss him to the ground, rip off his clothes, and spend the entire night making love to him. That would have been a huge mistake, and she couldn't afford any mistakes right now. So, the kiss had been gentle and brief. Maybe someday, when she figured a way out of this mess, she could come back, see if this crazy thing she felt for him went anywhere.

A nice dream, Kayla, but highly improbable.

Slinging the backpack over her shoulder, she very quietly opened the bedroom door. She half-expected it to squeak and give her away like some cheesy horror movie. It didn't.

After a quick glance around, she crept out of the room and down the hallway. She wished she could leave a note, but she didn't dare. Not only did she not want to leave a trail, but she also didn't want Ryder to get involved in her mess. He might be the sheriff, but Kayla was starting to believe he was one of the good guys. Not a crooked cop like David. Ryder was kind, caring, and ethical. He was the real deal.

The thick hallway runner muted her bootsteps as she made her way toward the front door. Her red winter coat still hung on the hook where she'd seen it earlier.

Almost free.

Dueling emotions racked her body—the need to leave warred with the desire to stay.

"Going somewhere?"

Kayla screamed, whirling around in attack mode. Her fists hit a hard, solid chest, and she shoved.

He found me! David found me, and now he's going to kill me, too.

All her terrified mind could think was to fight. She punched with all her might, but two very strong hands grasped her wrists and pulled, twisting her until her back slammed flat against her assailant's chest.

"Calm down you fool woman. It's me."

She stopped struggling. "Ryder?"

"Who the hell else did you think it would be?"

His voice grumbled, sending strange vibrations through her body. His arm brushed against her cheek as he reached beyond her and flipped on the light. She squinted against the brightness filling the room.

Though her pulse still pounded in her ears, embarrassment replaced fear. "What in the world are you doing? Trying to give me a heart attack?"

"No." The single word was a low growl in her ear. "I was waiting to catch you sneaking away."

She tipped her head to the side, caught red-handed; time to bluff her way out. "I wasn't sneaking out."

One dark eyebrow rose in disbelief, but he didn't let her go.

"I was thirsty."

"You always need a backpack full of stolen clothes and a winter parka for a glass of water, sweetheart?"

Sweetheart?

"I was going to return them," she mumbled, turning her face away to tuck her chin into her chest. "As soon as I get everything figured out."

His warm breath fanned over the back of her neck, sending shivers down her spine.

"What's to figure? Thought you didn't remember anything."

Shoot! She knew she'd slip up if she stayed long enough. His fault. He could have just let her leave.

"It's better if you don't know." She shook her head, fighting back tears.

"Why don't you let me be the judge of that?"

Ryder was so kind, so good. No way would she drag him into her mess. She was a wanted woman. He was the sheriff. If she stayed here, told him what happened, there were two outcomes. One—he would hand her over. Not acceptable. Or, two—he would try to help her and jeopardize his job, his freedom, and his life for her, a complete stranger. Also not acceptable.

"I can't drag you into my problems. Just let me go."

Long strands of his silky, dark hair fell over her shoulder as he leaned his head against hers and…

Did he brush his lips against my ear?

"I can't do that, Kayla. I'm the sheriff. It's my job to help people in trouble, and, sweetheart, from what I can see, you are in a big pile of it."

There he went with the sweetheart stuff again. She had no idea what that was all about, but he wasn't wrong. She *was* in a big pile of trouble. A landfill.

"Please, let me help you."

She wanted to. More than anything, she wanted to turn around, tell this strong, sweet man all her troubles and let him make them disappear. But she couldn't. It wouldn't be fair or safe. David was crazy. He would come looking for her, personally. If he found out Ryder helped her, there was no telling what he would do to keep his secret.

No, she had to solve this problem on her own. "It's not safe."

"I'm the sheriff of this town. It's my job to handle dangerous situations."

Still pinned against his chest, she felt the hard edges of his muscles, such a contrast to his comforting hold. The strong beat of his heart against her back settled her own into a synchronized rhythm.

Her breath caught in her throat, but not from fear this time. "But I'm not a part of this town. You have no obligation to help me. You don't even know me."

Silence.

Just when she thought she'd gotten through to him, that he was going to let her leave, his voice came as a soft, sensual caress. Dark, like chocolate, and just as tempting.

"I know it's crazy, but there's a part of me that feels like I've known you forever. Like I've been waiting for you. There's something between us, don't deny it. I know you feel it, too."

She sucked in a sharp breath. Yes, she did feel it. She hadn't realized *he* did. It was crazy and unexpected, but it was there. A connection apparently neither could deny. It terrified her even as it thrilled her. Unfortunately, this whole thing made her situation that much harder.

"Talk to me, Kayla," he whispered in her ear. "Let me help you."

Whatever powers that be—God, the Universe, or Aliens—that had led her to this man, they knew there was a reason she needed to meet him now, at this point in her life.

Maybe he wouldn't turn her in. Maybe he would be the one to help her. David may be a cop...but so was Ryder. Could he help her find evidence to prove her innocence? That was his job, after all, solving crimes. Maybe she *could* trust him. Trust this insane feeling she

48

got whenever he was near.

Taking a deep, shaky breath, and a giant leap of faith, she stepped out of his arms and turned, staring directly into those intelligent, warm eyes. "My name is Kayla Jenkins, and I'm wanted by the Chicago Police Department for the murder of my roommate, Jennifer Wright."

Chapter 7

Of all the things she could have said, *wanted for murder* would have been the last guess on Ryder's list. He knew she was in trouble, but he figured some small thing like petty theft or running from an ex. Never in a million years would he have pegged sweet, innocent looking Kayla as a murderer.

The devil was an angel once, too. Evil wears many masks.

Glancing at the small woman in front of him, he doubted an evil killer lurked inside. True, he knew nothing about her, but he had instincts. Good instincts. And they told him this woman could never kill another human being, at least, not in cold blood. Perhaps it had been an accident?

Then why did she run?

"I didn't do it." Her soft voice cracked with so many emotions, sadness, anger, fear…

Grasping her hand, he led her to the living room. A large recliner and a leather loveseat filled the room. Though he would have liked to sit next to her—comfort her as she so obviously needed—Ryder knew he had to keep his wits about him for this confession. Sitting in close contact to Kayla, touching her soft, velvety skin would muddle his brain for sure.

He instructed her to sit on the couch while he took a seat on the recliner facing her. Time to get answers.

All of them. "Tell me everything."

She took a deep breath. "I live outside of Chicago with my best friend, Jen. I mean...I did...live with Jen."

He watched as her eyes shuttered and filled with tears, but she blinked them back, obviously pulling on strength from somewhere deep inside her to push on.

"Jen and I met in college. We were roommates our sophomore year. She was in the nursing program, I was in early childhood education."

"You're a teacher?"

She nodded. "Kindergarten."

Grabbing a pencil and notepad lying on the coffee table, he asked, "Where?"

Her body stiffened at his poised position, but she set her jaw and answered. "Bishop Hills Elementary. It's a small magnet school in the city."

He wrote it down so he could check it out later. She might not like it, but he was going to check her story. If she wanted his help, he would need all the facts, listed and verified.

"Go on."

She pursed her lips then continued. "I came home from work on Friday. Jen was supposed to be home, but when I opened the apartment door I felt..." She tapered off, her eyes going hazy, face pale as a sheet.

Softly, he touched her hand, bringing her back to the present, keeping his voice as gentle as possible. "What?"

"I don't know." She shifted on the couch. "Off. I can't explain it really, but sometimes I get these strange feelings that something is wrong."

He understood. His gut had saved him many times

51

over the years.

"I called out to Jen, but she didn't answer, so I went to her room to check on her."

He watched her eyes glaze over—she was back there, in that apartment where something horrible happened, seeing what she described.

"Jen is—was—a very neat person." She choked a bit on the words but continued. "She always made her bed. Said it was a nurse habit from making so many at work. But when I went into her room, the bed was a mess, like someone had been rolling around on it. Things were knocked over. A lamp was broken. And then I slipped in something." Her hand flew up to her mouth as she tried unsuccessfully to hold back a sob.

Screw this. Rising from his chair, he set the pad and pencil on the coffee table again. He couldn't distance himself, not when she was so clearly hurting.

The cushion sank as he took the seat beside her on the loveseat. Without a word, she turned into his chest. He wrapped his arms around her in a comforting hug. "I know this is difficult, sweetheart, but I need you to tell me the rest."

She sniffed, wiping her tears on his shirt. "When I looked at what I slipped in, all I saw was red. So much red. And then I saw Jen. She was lying there on the floor. Her eyes were open, but she, they didn't look right."

The eyes of the dead. He'd seen them too often in his vocation. Blank, cold, wide open, but seeing nothing. You never forgot those eyes once you saw them. Never.

"I tr-tried to help, but it was t-t-too late." Sobs racked her body as she valiantly tried to finish her story. "There was b-b-blood in her hair...and her head, it looked like someone had smashed it in with something."

A burglary gone wrong? Wouldn't be the first time a homeowner had caught a thief in the act. Most panicked and ran, but some snapped and killed. "Was anything missing?"

Soft hair grazed his chin when she shook her head. "I know what you're thinking. I thought that, too, at first, but it wasn't a burglary."

"How do you know?"

"Because...the killer was still there."

"What?" Ryder's blood turned cold. Kayla had been in the house with the killer? She could have been hurt, killed.

He could have lost her before he even found her.

"David Tyler, Jen's boyfriend. At first, I was glad to see him. I thought he could help. I asked him how he got in. We always lock our door."

Two young women living alone together, they were smart to do so.

Her body trembled in his arms. "He said Jen gave him a key...which she would never do without discussing with me first."

"I take it she didn't discuss it with you?"

She shook her head. "That was when I noticed the bathroom door was open, and his shirt was wet." Her head lifted from his chest, and she glanced up at him, her eyes hard. "David is a police officer with the Chicago PD."

No wonder she freaked out when he mentioned he was the sheriff. If David had killed Jen, it made him a crooked cop, and tampering with evidence to point the crime away from him would be no problem for someone like that. Unfortunately, the badge didn't mean the same thing to everyone. Corruption happened.

"Cleaning up after the fact?"

A nod. "That's what I realized." Her breath shuddered out. "I knew David had a bit of a temper. Jen talked about it sometimes, but I never imagined he'd get so angry he would hurt her or—" Her words cut off as another sob escaped her.

Tucking her in close, he rubbed her back while rocking gently. "It's okay, sweetheart. Everything is going to be fine."

"No, it won't!" Her face shone red with anger as she pulled away. "David told me he was going to blame the whole thing on me. He made up this bunk story about how I was jealous of Jen and killed her in a fit of envy. He said his chief would never believe my word over his, and he could easily manipulate the evidence to cover his story." Leaping up, she paced. "Don't you see? He's a *cop*, of course everyone will believe him over me."

"He's a *bad* cop."

"Yeah, but no one knows that."

"You do, and if you let me help you, everyone else will, too."

The pacing stopped. She glanced at him, those blue-green eyes glossing over with tears of anger and despair. Damn, she was beautiful.

"I can help you. We'll dig into his past, look into the crime scene report, find something that proves what an evil bastard he is."

"How can we do that from so far away? Without anyone noticing?"

Peak Town may be a one-stoplight place, but he was still the sheriff. He had connections, friends in high places he worked with over the years. There were ways of getting information.

"You let me worry about that."

She took a tentative step toward him. "I don't want to put you in any danger. You could lose your job, or David might come after me and—"

Standing, he took the two steps separating them and placed his finger over her lips. "My job is to uphold the law and bring in the bad guy. You are not the bad guy. As for David, let him come. If that jackass so much as shows his face in my town, I'll haul him down to the station and throw him in a six by eight until he confesses."

Beautiful hazel eyes stared at him; her brow wrinkled. "I don't understand."

"What don't you understand?"

"Why are you helping me?" Her hands twisted together. "This is crazy. Why do you believe me? For all you know, I could be playing you."

He couldn't stop the chuckle rising up in his chest. "First of all, if you were playing me, why would you tell me about it? And second, judging by this ill-attempted escape tonight, I'd hardly peg you as a criminal mastermind."

When she started to protest again, he held up a hand. "I *can* help you. I promise. You have to promise me one thing, though."

She inched back with caution. "What?"

Not letting her escape, he gently grasped the back of her neck and pulled her toward him again. "You can't run, Kayla. If I'm going to help you, and I am,

55

you have to stay here where I can protect you. And I'm going to need complete honesty at all times. Can you do that?"

He waited and watched the play of emotions cross her face: fear, wariness, unease, and deep down underneath them all, a sliver of hope.

Finally, she nodded. "Yes, I can do that."

His shoulders sagged with relief. Leaning forward, he placed a soft kiss on her forehead. "Good. Now, I need you to go back to bed and get a good night sleep. We have a lot of work to do tomorrow."

She hesitated, worrying her bottom lip with her teeth. "I still don't understand why you're helping me, but thank you, Ryder."

Confusion and hope swirled in those hazel eyes before she turned and started back down the hall to her room.

She was still wary of his help. That much was clear. Hell, so was he. As an officer of the law, he should have called Chicago PD the moment she revealed herself to be a fugitive. He was putting his career, and his very freedom, at stake for a woman he'd known less than forty-eight hours.

But his gut was talking to him, telling him she was innocent. Being framed by a bad cop with no respect for the badge—he *hated* guys like that. They gave all the good cops a bad name. He got into this field so he could make a difference, catch the bad guys, make sure justice was served. He'd be damned if he let this David guy get away with murder.

Tomorrow, he'd call his sister. If anyone could dig up dirt on someone it was Julie. Then he'd call some of his old buddies from the police academy. Liam was with the FBI now. Crazy bastard owed him a favor or two.

Ryder stared down the hall as the guest room door closed with a soft click.

Time to call one in.

Chapter 8

"Tyler, what you doing here, man?"

David Tyler ran a hand over his face, trying to hide his smug grin. It was the fourth time one of his fellow officers had asked him that. "I can't sit at home anymore." He injected a hint of despair in his tone.

The standard reply he'd been giving everyone seemed to be appeasing the masses concerned with his mourning. Three days had passed since his little screw up with Jen.

Little screw up? More like giant shit storm thanks to little Ms. Nosy Pants.

He hadn't meant to kill Jen. It just sort of…happened. Sometimes he forgot his own strength. The whole incident wasn't his fault, really. It was hers. She shouldn't have been flirting with that smarmy-ass doctor. She was *his* woman.

Disrespecting, bitch.

She'd needed a lesson on how to behave when she belonged to *him*, so he'd given it to her.

His family held a lot of respect in the community. With his father's City Council job and his mother's charity work, the public was always scrutinizing his family. Scandals were not tolerated in the Tyler household. Jen knew that. Affairs were lapped up by the press. Sure, she said they were just coworkers, but he knew better. He'd seen them together, talking, laughing…touching. Jen tried to pass it off as a friendly touch of the arm. Social norms or some crap.

Bullshit!

He knew a come on when he saw it. Anger had burned, furious and righteously in his gut when he saw pretty-boy doctor touch *his* woman. He wanted to rip the guy's head off and shove it up his ass. But fighting a respected neurosurgeon would create a scandal. And since he couldn't get his satisfaction by beating the hell out of the damned doc, he taught Jen a thing or two about respect.

"Never let a woman play you for a fool, son."

Wise words his father always told him. And he was nobody's fool.

He'd repeated those same words to Jen when she'd been crying and begging him to stop. But he hadn't stopped. The rage had been too great, the vindication too strong. She needed to be taught a lesson, and he had to be the one to teach it to her. The lamp just sort of ended up in his hand; he didn't remember how. When he brought it down on her head, the screams and begging had stopped. It took him a few minutes to realize Jen was dead.

She deserved what she got. Lying, cheating bitch.

He figured he had time to clean up, make it look like a burglary gone wrong. Then her stupid roommate had come home.

He never liked Kayla, a nobody who worked with smelly kids all day. He hated kids. But what he really hated about her was the close relationship she and Jen shared. He could never get Jen to agree to any-*fucking*-thing until she talked it over with her best friend.

"Let's go to Mexico next month."

"I have to talk to Kayla first."
"I want a key to your place."
"I have to talk to Kayla first."
Annoying as shit.

He almost lost his head when he came out of the bathroom and saw her holding Jen's body. Stupid bitch was supposed to be at school. Why had she come home early?

She ruined everything!

For a moment, he'd thought he could still pass off the burglar story, but Kayla hadn't bought it. The teacher had a few working brain cells. Smarter than Jen had been. Bitch had morals, too. Once, he offered to help take care of a parking ticket for her, and she refused. Said it wasn't right to take advantage of the system that way.

Fucking Dana-Do-Right.

Taking advantages was one of the whole reasons he became a cop. What was the point of having power if you didn't use it to your benefit? Another important lesson instilled in him by his father—a powerful man in his own right who knew how to wield it.

He'd known there was no way he could pay Kayla off to keep her mouth shut. She believed in doing "the right thing." Plus, she never really liked him much. Oh, she'd love to see him put behind bars. But that wasn't happening. No way would he let himself be thrown in some dirty-ass cell with a bunch of thugs. Most he'd put away.

He wouldn't survive a week.

"Hey, man, you all right?"

Shaking himself out of his thoughts, David looked up to see Steve Carlyle and Jim Foster. Two officers he'd worked with a few times over the years. Okay guys.

"Yeah, I'm hanging in."

They gave him a sympathetic pat on the shoulder as they walked by.

God, this was almost too easy. Everyone was eating up this "wounded boyfriend" shit. Concocting the story about Kayla killing Jen in a jealous rage had been a stroke of pure genius. As he told the pathetic little teacher, she was a nobody with no family. Who would take her word over his, a respected cop?

Would have been better if he could have gotten rid of her, too. He didn't like the fact she was out there somewhere, possibly telling people what happened. He didn't think anyone would believer her. She was wanted for murder—who would believe her? Every guilty person claimed they were innocent.

Still, it would be better if he found her before his chief did. Take her out before she got a chance to talk. He didn't want anyone looking into Jen's death too closely. His story would hold. The evidence would support him, he made sure of that. But if people started looking too closely, they might find holes. He had to plug those holes, ASAP.

The squeak of rubber soles on hard linoleum caused him to look up. Jim had come back, dumbass pity still in the guy's eyes.

"Chief Vic wants to see you."

"On my way there now."

David paused before the door, taking a moment to sink into grieving boyfriend mode. The chief sat at his desk as he entered the small office. The old man looked up when the door closed with a soft click.

Chief Charlie Vickers—or Chief Vic as everyone referred to him—eyed him with something as close to sympathy as the hardened cop could. Forty years on the force had made the chief stone. The old guy had seen a lot in his day and didn't take crap from anyone. He was a good man to work for. Not crooked; but he never dug too deep into any of his men's cases, so David could work with that. The chief had a "don't ask, don't tell" type policy, of which he took full advantage.

"David, I'm glad you came in today. I wanted to talk to you."

He had been given three day's paid leave. Standard procedure. Suited him fine; nothing like getting paid to sit on your ass drinking beer and watching football for three days.

"I wanted to talk to you, too, Chief."

His boss dug out a wad of chew and stuck it in his bottom lip. Nasty habit, but he didn't begrudge a man his vices.

"Look," the old man started. "I know you want to go after Kayla Jenkins, but I don't think that's such a good idea."

"She killed the woman I love, sir."

"That's exactly the reason you shouldn't go after her." The cracked leather office chair groaned as he sat back. Too many years behind a desk had given the old guy a gut to rival Jolly Old Saint Nick. Not that anyone would call Vickers jolly. He'd probably lock them in a six by eight for a week.

"You're too emotionally involved. I can't let you work on this case."

He had to work on this case. He needed to know everything that was going on. Every bit of evidence collected, every lead found, and any sighting of Kayla. He *needed* to find her first.

Find her and silence her.

For good.

"I need to be on this case, sir. Please." He sniffed, trying to appear as if he was holding back tears, knowing any type of emotions were uncomfortable for the old guy.

Must have been pretty convincing because Vic shifted in his seat. "I guess I can let you in," his boss conceded.

I should get a friggin' Oscar.

"But you need to work with a partner. Someone to keep you in line so you don't go all Dirty Harry on me."

Shit. It'd be a lot harder to make sure everything got covered up with a partner breathing down his neck. Of course, if he got the right partner…

"Fair enough, but can I choose the guy?"

Chief Vic stared at him, his face hard, but nodded.

"I want Foster." Jim was a guy who'd look the other way for enough cash. They had worked together enough for him to know the other man's price. A price he would happily pay.

The chief inclined his head. "Done."

"Thank you, sir."

"Let me know the second you find anything." A stubby, tobacco-stained finger pointed. "And don't you even think of going after that girl on your own. I don't want a vengeance killing on top of everything else. You find her and report back to me. Got it?"

"Yes, sir."

"Dismissed."

The stupid old fart bought every lie that fell out of his mouth. No surprise. Lying came easy to David. Just like his old man. Must be genetic.

He left the chief's office to find Foster, lay down the score, and get to work. While Jim made sure nothing in the evidence pointed to him, David would find that bitch. Then he'd call the chief…right after he made sure Ms. Kayla Jenkins had a terrible, life-ending accident.

Chapter 9

The smell of bacon woke Kayla again. Her stomach growled, eager for the salty, delicious meat. As a teacher, she had to arrive at school an hour before the students. Since classes started at seven in the morning, she'd get up at five in order to get ready and be to work on time. No one wanted to cook at five am. Most days, she would grab a banana or quick bowl of cold cereal. Having bacon and eggs every morning was nice.

Too nice to get used to.

Groaning, she slumped deeper into the covers. She had to remember why she was here. She still couldn't believe she told Ryder the truth last night. Not like he gave her much of a choice. Truthfully, she was glad he caught her sneaking out. Her only plan had been to run, take her problems with her, and away from him. She'd had no idea what to do next or how she would prove David's guilt.

She sighed as the tight band of pressure around her chest eased. Ryder not only believed her, he promised to help. It amazed her. He was the sheriff. Sworn to uphold the law. By that logic, she should be sitting in a cell right now waiting for the Chicago PD to come haul her back to Illinois for a murder trial. But she wasn't. She was lying in his guest bed, smelling the delicious breakfast he made for her, again. Waiting for him to help her solve her problems.

Why?

She still didn't fully understand why this man would risk everything for her, a woman he barely knew.

"There's a part of me that feels like I've known you forever. That I've been waiting for you."

It should have sounded like such a practiced line. Would have, if she hadn't felt the exact same thing. The strange connection they seemed to share...she felt it, too.

Or maybe all this running for your life is making you delirious.

While she knew she couldn't afford to trust anyone, she placed her trust in Ryder. Why? The man was her only option at the moment, true, but was there more to it? Somewhere deep inside, did she know he would protect her?

A dull ache pounded in her head. Her emotions were too messy for her to decipher. She would just have to put her trust in the Universe, and Ryder, for the moment. It thrilled and terrified her all at the same time.

A soft knock on the door interrupted her thoughts.

"Kayla? Are you up yet?"

His deep voice sent chills racing up and down her body. "Yes," she said, embarrassed when her voice squeaked. She cleared her throat and tried again. "Yes, I'm up."

"Breakfast is almost ready. Come on out whenever you're dressed."

Dressed. That reminded her. She needed clothes. Julie Ryder's were fine yesterday, but they weren't exactly the same size. The pants cut closer to capris on her, and while she wouldn't call herself a large woman, she was much *bustier* than Ryder's sister. The sweater yesterday clung a little tighter than she preferred. Also, she needed a bra and some underwear. Commando wasn't really her style. If she would be staying here until they figured this whole thing out, she needed to get some clothes of her own.

Her pulse raced at the thought of going into town. What if someone recognized her from a news broadcast? Ordering clothes online would take too long, and she'd thrown all her cards and identification away when her wanted poster had been splashed across the five o'clock news. The cash she pulled from her bank account before running was slowly dwindling, but she had enough to purchase a few things.

Her stomach grumbled again, reminding her of the scrumptious smelling breakfast waiting for her. Throwing off the covers, she quickly dressed in a pair of jeans, a blue T-shirt, and a lovely lilac sweater so soft and warm she never wanted to take it off. Ryder's sister had great taste in clothes. Maybe someday they could go shopping together.

Stupid! You are not here on vacation.

She was on the run for murder. The only thing she and Julie would be doing together would be facing a judge when the woman represented her during the murder trial. Except the woman was a prosecutor. So, it would be more likely she'd be the one trying to put her in jail.

Stop it, Kayla. Ryder said he and his sister would help. Have some faith.

She made her way into the kitchen, clearing her throat to announce her presence. Ryder turned from his position at the stove and smiled. "There you are. I was beginning to worry you'd snuck out the window."

Kayla self-consciously tucked her new shorter hair behind her ear. "I said I would stay."

He smiled. "You did."

"I was thinking as I was getting dressed…"

"Yes?"

"I, um, can't keep borrowing your sister's clothes." When he opened his mouth, no doubt to protest, she rushed to explain. "It's very kind of you to let me, but we're not quite the same size, and besides, I need…um, that is…I don't have any…"

Oh goodness, this shouldn't be so awkward. Everyone wears underwear.

Her face heated. Why was her body reacting this way? Maybe because mentioning bras and panties in Ryder's presence made her mind conjure up *other* things. Things involving him *removing* said underclothes right before he laid her down on a soft bed and—

"Kayla?"

She realized she was breathing heavily, and from the hot flush, she was sure her face had gone beyond a blush into bright red territory.

Oh goodness, can I be any more of a dork?

Ryder basically caught her having a wet daydream about him. In his kitchen! With bacon sizzling on the stove and coffee brewing. What was wrong with her? She felt like the fifth grade girls at her school after they watch the "Your Body and New Feelings" video that was part of the health curriculum.

"I need underwear." The words tumbled from her lips.

He dipped his head as if trying to hide a smile. Well, at least he found it amusing. She wanted to crawl in the nearest hole and stay there until the next ice age. Which, from a glance out the kitchen window, might not be too far off.

Like the gentleman he was, he ignored her embarrassment. "We can drive into town today to do some shopping. I need to check in at the station anyway."

She sat at the table where a steaming cup of coffee waited. Ryder placed a plate of scrambled eggs, toast, and bacon in front of her. The delicious aromas had her stomach growling with anticipation.

Kayla took a bite of the eggs, and *oh my*, it was like heaven in her mouth. The enjoyment didn't last long when her brain went back to the risk of going into town. Taking a second bite, the eggs still tasted wonderful, but her stomach tuned over. She pushed the food around her plate, biting her lip. "Do you think that's wise? What if someone recognizes me?"

Ryder finished chewing the enormous bite in his mouth before answering. "I doubt anyone will recognize you. Peak Town is a small community. We don't get much crime report from outside of Colorado. Unless it's something major."

Wanted for murder seems pretty major.

"Plus, it looks like you tried to remedy that problem already. Am I right?" He pointed to her sad attempt at a haircut.

Embarrassed, she fiddled with the choppy strands and nodded. "Yes. When I saw a report for my arrest, I went to a drug store and got some hair dye. I also cut it myself. I know it looks hideous, but I'm too recognizable with my natural hair."

"What is your natural hair color?" His eyes lit with

curiosity.

She sighed, lamenting her lost locks. "A coppery red...and halfway down my back. I'd been growing it for years."

Chocolate brown eyes flared with heat as he sucked in a sharp breath. "I'm sorry you had to cut it."

So was she, especially now

"But you were right to do so," he continued. "Hair that unique would certainly be recognizable."

Kayla took a sip of her coffee and thought she heard him mumble under his breath, *"Red, sonofabitch!"*

She was used to men's reactions to her hair. It had garnered a few spontaneous proposals even. Something about redheads made men go crazy. It was silly, and she usually ignored it, but the reaction coming from Ryder felt different. The way his eyes dilated, filled with hunger despite the huge plate of food in front of him, caught her off guard. The mention of her natural hair seemed to awaken something wild and ravenous in him.

And exhilarated her.

Down girl. The man is helping you out of a jam, not your clothes.

"So, you think a trip into town would be okay? I have cash. I threw all my credit cards away."

"So they couldn't trace you?"

She nodded.

"Smart."

"To quote my students, 'I saw it on TV.' All those nights sitting grading on the couch while watching crime shows finally paid off, I guess." She shrugged, her cheeks heating with embarrassment when he chuckled.

"We'll head into town after breakfast. After a quick trip to the station, we can go shopping for clothes."

When he rose to refill his mug, Kayla stared at her half-eaten plate. The delicious food no longer seemed as appetizing. She couldn't avoid town forever, but to go to the police station? Didn't they hang wanted posters in there? Ryder said the small town didn't get much crime reports from out of state, but what if they had this time? What if her picture was hung all over the station? They'd lock her up and throw away the key— *he'd* have to. That was his job.

"Kayla?"

Ryder's voice came to her through her fog of panic.

"Everything will be okay, sweetheart. I promise. You trust me, right?"

She took a deep, calming breath, stared into his mesmerizing dark eyes, and nodded, because for some inexplicable reason, she did.

Chapter 10

Kayla was in the kitchen cleaning up the breakfast dishes. At her persistence. Ryder told her she didn't need to clean up, but the sweet, stubborn woman had insisted on helping. Something about trying to pay him back for his kindness.

Ridiculous.

He wasn't doing anything for her any good cop wouldn't do. Okay, maybe he was helping her out by *not* turning her in. She was a wanted woman, but he suspected she was being framed, and that did not sit well with him at all. He'd seen a frame job or two in his time. Horrible when people twisted the law to condemn innocent people. Innocent until proven guilty was a saying he took to heart. And he would discover if Kayla was innocent or guilty, no matter what strange feelings he had for her.

Last night after her revelation, he went online to look into her story. He believed her, but what kind of cop would he be if he didn't verify the facts for himself? Not a very good one. The police database would raise too many red flags, so he stuck to web searches. There was plenty of information on the murder of Jennifer Wright. It happened just as Kayla said, even down to David Tyler pointing the finger at her. She appeared to be telling the truth, but most criminals claimed they were setup. As much as he wanted to put all his faith in her, he needed more evidence.

While she was occupied in the kitchen, he snuck off to his bedroom and put in a call to his buddy in the FBI. "Hey, Liam."

"Jake Ryder! As I live and breathe. How's the polar ice caps, my man?"

The agent visited Peak Town for New Year's last year. Whiney bastard was still complaining. "It wasn't *that* cold, you wuss."

The other man's snort came through the phone line. "I damn near lost an ear to frostbite."

Ryder chuckled at the exaggeration. Liam was originally from Florida—the man thought anything below seventy was freezing. "Good thing you didn't. Then you'd have a hole in the side of your head, and that sorry excuse you call a brain would fall right out."

"At least I have my good looks. Which is more than I can say for your ugly mug."

They'd hassled each other like crazy in the academy. Some things never changed. Liam was one of the few guys Ryder had really connected with there. It was times like this he really missed the smartass bastard.

"What do you want, Nanook of the North?"

"I'm calling in a favor."

His friend's teasing edge dropped. "What do you need?"

"Some background information on a guy named David Tyler, a cop from Chicago."

There was a pause, then the deep voice came back over the line. "He dirty?"

"Might be. That's what I need to find out."

"I'll pick through his file with a fine toothed comb." The dark words came out in a growl.

That was why he liked Liam so much. The guy hated dirty cops as much as he did. His buddy was a good guy, true and blue. He didn't suffer cheaters or liars. Bad cops held a special place in Liam's ass-kicking department. Ryder never asked why. He wasn't sure he wanted to know.

"Thanks, man." He knew his friend would find the information he needed without arousing suspicion. Liam was good like that.

After a bit more good-natured ribbing back, Ryder said goodbye to his friend and walked back into the kitchen.

Kayla had finished the dishes and was grabbing her coat off the rack. "Are you all set?"

She didn't ask where he had gone or what he'd been doing. He could still see the question in her beautiful hazel eyes, but she didn't ask. The woman was placing her trust in him, her life. A humbling feeling.

He nodded, grabbing for his coat and cowboy hat. A frigid blast of air hit him square in the face when he opened the front door. He tugged the collar of his jacket higher and turned to Kayla. "It's damn near freezing outside, but the truck has a great heater." A requirement he spared no expense on when he bought the large vehicle a few years back. "Should get us toasty warm in no time."

She shivered against the cold wind that blew inside the doorway. "You have a truck?"

"Sure. You didn't think I rode Wind Chaser everywhere did you?" He smiled at her sheepish expression. She was cute when she got embarrassed. "I know Peak Town is kind of out in the boonies, but we do live in the twenty-first century. We have Wi-Fi and everything."

She rolled her eyes. A smile tilted her lips, the first real full one he'd seen. It was fun teasing Kayla, and he was thankful he could ease some of her worry. The poor woman had gone through such a tragic event. No one should have to see someone they loved after such a brutal death. He knew Kayla had loved her roommate, Jen—it was in the way she talked about the deceased woman. The same way Ryder spoke of his sister, with special fondness. He could only imagine how horrible it must have been to come home, expecting to see your best friend happy and alive, but instead, find her lifeless body lying on the ground covered in blood.

Horrifying.

As a cop, he had seen his fair share of horrific accidents, gruesome murders, and tragic crime scenes. But he never knew any of those people on a personal level. All the major crime he saw had been during his stint in the city. Denver was fairly safe for a big city, but it had its share of corruption. After a few years as a beat cop, witnessing the death and cruelty too common to city life, he decided to come home to Peak Town.

He got a job on the force right away. Not hard to do since there were only two officers at the time. When Sheriff Hensley retired, Ryder ran for the position, unopposed. He took care of his town, and they appreciated it.

But, while he dealt with death, had seen some pretty terrible stuff, he'd never seen something as horrifying as what Kayla described. And now, she had to deal with being blamed for the crime. It all seemed too much for one person to bear, but she was holding up like a champ. He saw the moments she almost broke, and how she pulled herself back together. She fought through her pain to bring her friend's killer to justice, even though she was terrified for her own life. Her strength amazed him. Which was why he was determined to help her.

"So, how far is town?"

Kayla's soft voice broke through his thoughts, bringing him back to the present as they made their way to the truck. "Not far. About fifteen minutes. A lot of people live outside of the town proper. There's a lot of ranch property out here."

Using the thick sleeve of his jacket, he brushed the snow off the driver side door before opening it and leaning in to insert the keys in the ignition. He turned the heater full blast, making the interior nice and warm then instructed Kayla to sit in the cab while he cleared the snow off the vehicle. She tried to argue, but this time, he did the insisting. His mama would roll over in her grave if he let a woman freeze her butt off clearing his truck. Besides, it didn't take too long.

The streets had been plowed yesterday, but a fresh snow had fallen overnight, leaving about an inch on the road. Not a big deal. He'd driven in worse. At least the road to his place was paved.

Just like he told her, it was about fifteen minutes before they arrived in town. He headed to the station first to check in. As sheriff, he was technically on call at all times. The force had grown since he started. He now employed a dozen men and women. Their numbers were still smaller than he'd like, but the crime in Peak

Town was miniscule, so they made do. Everyone was scheduled for two days off a week. Today was the end of his "weekend," but he liked to check in anyway to make sure nothing needed his immediate attention. Plus, he wanted to check if the news of Jennifer Wright's murder had hit Peak Town.

Pulling into the station parking lot, he glanced at Kayla. As she realized where they were, she went pale. He saw the fine tremor rack her body even though the truck was warm and she still had her winter coat on. She was scared. Hell, why wouldn't she be? She'd spent the last few days running from the authorities, and here he was bringing her to the one place she feared the most.

I am an ass.

"Hey." He gently touched a finger to her chin. She turned her head toward him, eyes wide with distress. "Shit, come here." He pulled her across the bench seat, unclicking her seat belt so he could wrap an arm around her. "I know this is the last place you want to be."

"I just—what if someone recognizes me?"

"Like I said, Peak Town doesn't get much outside news." He tucked her into his shoulder, and surprisingly, she let him. She buried her face in his chest, seeking comfort, and hell if he didn't want to give it to her. Damn, what this woman did to him.

"I doubt the news about what happened in Chicago will be in our office." Still, there *was* an outside possibility they had gotten the APB. Perhaps she shouldn't go into the station. "How about I go in, and you wait here for me in the truck?"

She pulled her head off his chest and glanced up. The gratitude in her eyes nearly did him in.

"But you have to stay in the truck." He stared at her. "No running."

She nodded. "No running."

Could he trust her? He had to. She trusted him, to a degree. This was a shaky game they were playing. Two strangers placing such blind faith in each other.

"Okay, I'll be in and out. Ten minutes."

He made it in eight. After saying hello to the desk clerk, Mrs. Billings—a nice woman of sixty who had been running the sheriff's station since well before his time—he checked in with his deputy, Tim, who told him everything was fine. A plow broke down last night leading to a few calls from irate citizens who couldn't get out of their driveways, but they had called in Pete who ran the local auto body shop. He had a truck with a front plow and was always willing to help out.

Everything was business as usual. No news about a female killer from Chicago. Kayla was safe, for now.

After the station, he drove the five blocks to The Cowhand, the only clothing store in Peak Town. He hoped she liked denim and flannel.

The store was warm and mostly empty. Kayla chose her items in record time. Ryder was used to shopping with his sister. Julie loved clothes. She could spend hours sifting through the rack, trying on everything in the store. It gave him a headache every time. He never understood why women spent so much time picking out clothes. When he went shopping, he grabbed whatever fit and got out of there. Who cared if the jeans he bought were "last season." For forty bucks, they better last ten seasons.

They were about to leave the store when a friendly voice called out, "Ryder!"

He turned and practically got tackled by a hundred and sixty pounds of enthusiastic pregnant woman.

"Hey, Lizzy. How are you doing, sweetheart?"

At his use of the endearment, he heard Kayla suck in a sharp breath. He didn't have time to ponder over that because Lizzy, in typical fashion, jumped right in.

"I am doing great! Okay, well not great. The nausea is gone, but I'm starting to get huge and all my joints hurt. I have heartburn that could rival a bonfire, none of my clothes fit, and this town has absolutely nothing in the way of maternity clothing. It's making me frustrangry."

When she finally stopped to take a breath, he laughed. "Lizzy, that's not a word."

"Well, it should be." She paused in her tirade, gaze sliding to Kayla. "Oh, hello. Ryder, aren't you going to introduce me to your lady friend?" Her eyebrows waggled as she drew out the word "friend."

"Lizzy, this is my *friend* Kayla. Kayla, this is Elizabeth Hayworth."

"Soon to be Denning." The boisterous woman gave a warm smile. "Hopefully before I look too much like a bloated whale."

"You look lovely, Lizzy. Positively glowing."

She gave him a sideway glance. "You already get free cupcakes, Ryder, flattery will not get you free cookies."

"You guys are selling cookies now?"

"Just for the holidays. Kind of a special treat to get people in the door."

He rolled his eyes. "Yeah, like you need help getting people in the shop." Turning to Kayla—who looked lost as a fish in the woods—he explained,

"Lizzy and her friend, Maggie, run the cupcake shop in town."

"I do the business side, and Maggie does all the baking."

"Thankfully," he muttered under his breath.

Lizzy swatted his arm. "I heard that, Jake Ryder. No more cupcakes for you."

Grabbing her hand, he kissed it in apology. "I'm sorry. I didn't mean it."

The cheery woman shook her head, laughing. "Okay, you're forgiven." She grimaced, addressing Kayla. "It's true though. I once burned water. I'm a mess in the kitchen. That's why Maggie does the baking. Speaking of Maggie…she mentioned you were coming to dinner this week?"

Bright gray eyes danced as her gaze went back and forth between him and Kayla. He had promised Maggie when he saw her in town earlier this week, but that had been before Kayla and this situation. She wouldn't want anyone knowing who she was, making a group dinner out of the question.

Just as he was about to make an excuse, Lizzy spoke. "We'd love for you to come, too, Kayla."

Her mouth opened, but nothing came out. A smile curled his lips—Lizzy's energetic attitude did that to people. She was so outgoing and lively, it took some people off guard.

"I've never met you before, so I assume you're visiting Ryder from out of town?"

"Yes, I'm from back east." Her words were soft and hesitant.

Not a lie, he supposed. "She's only in town for a short time," he interjected, hoping to forestall more

80

questions. The poor woman had enough on her plate at the moment. She didn't need to deal with kindhearted, but nosy, inquiries.

"I see." Lizzy gave him a look that said she didn't see, but soon would.

Meddlesome woman.

He knew Lizzy wouldn't stop until she was satisfied.

"Well then, if you're visiting you must come to dinner. You can meet my fiancé, Dade, and his brother, Colton—Maggie's fiancé. She makes the best food you have ever tasted. Trust me, after a Maggie meal, you will feel like your taste buds have died and gone to heaven."

"Oh, um, sure. I'd—I'd love to."

Lizzy beamed. "Perfect! I'll tell the boys to expect a call from you, Ryder." She gave him a quick kiss on the cheek then embraced Kayla warmly. "So lovely to meet you. Can't wait to get to know you better."

With that, she pushed out the door, leaving the store and a very perplexed Kayla in her wake. If her situation weren't so dire, he would have laughed.

"Welcome to Peak Town. See, I told you there was nothing to worry about."

She turned to him with wide eyes. "Are you kidding? Now I'm worried there's something in the town's water. How can anyone be that energetic while pregnant?"

All the ugliness around her and she still kept her sense of humor. This woman was full of surprises. This time, he did laugh, and it warmed his heart to hear Kayla join in.

Chapter 11

"So, Lizzy and Maggie run a cupcake shop together and are engaged to brothers?" Kayla asked.

Once they left The Cowhand, Ryder suggested grabbing some lunch. He could tell she needed a moment to gather her thoughts. Most people did after an encounter with Lizzy. The woman was a whirlwind of energy.

"Yup." He could see her trying to puzzle out his relationship to the women in her head. "Maggie used to come out for the summers to stay with her gran. Moved out here last year to take over her grandmother's cupcake shop after she passed. Maggie and Colton were childhood friends, which developed into something more when she moved back. Maggie had some problems with a citizen who thought the shop shouldn't have gone to her. Tried to scare her off."

Kayla sucked in a sharp breath. "She was threatened?"

He nodded sadly. "More than—she was shot."

Kayla covered her mouth in horror.

Shoot! He hadn't meant to bring up bad memories.

"She's fine now," he added quickly. "We got the assailant responsible. But Maggie needed some help in the shop after that, so Lizzy came out to lend a hand. She and Colton's brother, Dade, kind of had an opposites attract thing going on. I've never seen two people so contrary, and so deeply in love."

Ellen came by to drop off their food. There were a few different eateries in Peak Town. Ryder had chosen Merle's Diner because it had great food, and he liked the proprietors.

"Thanks."

"Anytime, Sheriff."

The older woman eyed Kayla, but said nothing. Great, with the way this small town gossiped, her presence would be spread around before they finished their BLTs. He knew she wouldn't like that, but it couldn't be avoided. Besides, no one would be thinking she was a fugitive—they would be wondering who the sheriff's new squeeze was.

"How's Merle?" he asked, hoping to deflect the other woman's attention.

Ellen rolled her eyes good-naturedly. "Oh, you know Merle. Up at the crack of dawn to clear the sidewalks then right to the kitchen to slave over a hot stove. I keep telling the man he's not twenty anymore. He needs to slow down."

"I'll slow down when you do, ya old bat," a haggard voice shouted lovingly from the diner kitchen.

"Quiet, you old coot! Get back to work."

Ryder couldn't stop a wide grin from curling his lips. Merle and Ellen had owned the diner for years. They bickered constantly, but all in jest. They still acted like teenagers on prom night whenever they got within inches of each other. Hilarious to watch, and a big reason the diner was so popular.

"So, Sheriff." Ellen turned her attention back to the table. "Are you going to introduce me to your *friend?*"

The bite of food he'd taken went down the wrong

tube. The people in this town really needed to work on their subtlety. He coughed, taking a sip from his water to help the offending morsel down. Talking about Kayla was the last thing he should do, but he saw no escape for it.

"Ellen, this is Kayla. She's visiting from back east. Kayla, this is Ellen. She owns the diner along with her husband, Merle."

"The crazy old man in the back who made your food."

"I heard that woman!"

She winked.

Kayla smiled tentatively, clearly uncomfortable being singled out. "Well, it's delicious. Be sure to send him my appreciation."

Ellen snorted. "And inflate that giant ego of his? Not likely. I'll keep your praises to myself."

"I heard that, too!"

The feisty diner owner smiled, blowing a kiss toward the open windowed kitchen. Merle's wrinkled, smiling face popped out. His hand flew up to catch the air kiss then he smacked it right on his backside.

The laugh burst out of him before Ryder could stop it. Not that it would offend the two old timers; they loved to put on a show for their customers.

"Woman, please. We're in public." Mel waggled his brows, giving his wife a lusty look.

The older woman laughed. "Sixty-three years old and he still acts like a teenager." She shook her head, but the love there was obvious.

Deep in his gut something stirred, something that felt an awful lot like envy.

"So, Kayla, where did you meet our Sheriff

Ryder?"

His *friend* shifted in her seat. "Oh, um, we met at…uh…"

A rich laugh left the female proprietor's lips. "Oh, I'm sorry, sugar. I didn't mean to put you on the spot. I'm just so curious. The sheriff doesn't have many *female friends.*"

Again with the subtlety.

"I was hoping to get to know you before the rumor mill started."

"Rumor mill?" Kayla's brow drew down in confusion.

"Yes, dear. Small town, not much going on. New gal like you will be the talk of the town by dinnertime. There will be all kinds of speculation on who you are and what your relationship is to the sheriff."

The younger woman sucked in a sharp breath. Though he did tell her not to worry about being recognized in town, he probably should have mentioned everyone would be more interested in her relationship to *him*.

"Everything from a torrid love affair to a witness protection placement. On the run from murders who want you dead."

Ryder watched as all the color drained from Kayla's face. Ellen was only joking, but her jest hit too close to home. True, the town would be gossiping the moment they left the diner. Hell, by the looks of the table next to them, townsfolk hunched over in conversation, the rumor mill was already running.

"I thought I'd get the straight story first. That way I can set everyone else straight."

"And have the advantage of knowing the truth

before everyone else, right?" Ryder joked, trying to divert attention away from Kayla and set her nerves at ease. She looked like she was going to be ill.

Ellen laughed, patting him on the shoulder. "Right you are, hon."

"Well, we're just friends. Kayla happened to be in town, so she's staying at my place for a bit. So set the rumor mill to bed. Nothing scandalous going on here."

Mostly true.

"I'll do what I can, but you know this town." A patron raised a hand, catching Ellen's attention. "I better get back to work. You two have fun now." With a wink, the older woman departed.

Ryder glanced at Kayla; her hands trembled in her lap.

Dammit.

He never should have brought her into town. What had he been thinking?

"You okay?" The remainder of her half-eaten sandwich lay untouched on her plate. "Small towns like to gossip. Don't worry, the most people will think is that we're having a torrid love affair."

Her head snapped up, face flaming with embarrassment.

Shit. Why had he said that? It was true, most people would think they were lovers. He rarely dated and never had people stay with him, except for his sister. A single woman staying at his home would put ideas into people's heads. Hell, it was putting ideas into *his* head, ideas that should not be there. Kayla was scared and vulnerable. The last thing she needed was the man who vowed to protect her trying to get her into bed.

Tossing enough cash to cover the bill, and a hefty tip, on the table, he rose.

"You ready to head out?" They hadn't eaten much, but his appetite was gone, and judging by the way she hunched over, Kayla's was, too.

"Yes."

Ryder wanted to put her mind at ease, but he didn't know what else to say. The drive back to his place was quiet, the only sound filling the cab being the country music crackling over the radio. Reception wasn't always the best up in the mountains.

When they arrived back home, Kayla asked if she could use his washer and dryer for her new wardrobe. He showed her to the small laundry room off the kitchen. While she busied herself with laundry, he decided to shoot off a text to Liam, see if the man had dug up anything yet.

—Hey buddy. How's it going?—

A few moments later, his phone pinged with a reply.

—Boring as hell, but I'm keeping busy.—

Code for: he found nothing yet, but he was still looking. *Dammit.*

—Thinking of taking a vacation. Maybe somewhere down south, where it's warmer. I'll let you know.—

That meant Liam was going to start searching classified reports. No one liked to think about a cop going bad. Most people wouldn't admit it even if the evidence was right in front of them. There was something about the betrayal of someone tasked with the safety of citizens that really got to people. When checking into a dirty cop, it was best to do it under the wire until you had solid proof. No one wanted to accuse a good cop of bad deeds. That was a career destroyer.

Ryder believed Kayla's story, but if he was ever going to get anyone else to believe her, he had to have some evidence, some kind of proof of David's misdeeds. A violent kill like that didn't just happen. There had to be something in David Tyler's past leading up to it. Some show of anger, rage, viciousness. He gripped the phone tightly. It was there, he just had to find it.

"Ryder?"

Kayla's soft voice broke through his thoughts. "Hey."

"Everything okay?"

He rubbed a hand over his eyes, slipping his phone back into his pocket. "Yeah. I asked a friend to look into David. He hasn't found anything yet, but he's still looking."

She bit her lip, fingers fidgeting at her sides. "What are you hoping to find?"

"Something to show he's a dirty cop."

Hazel eyes filled with worry. "He might not be dirty. I mean, yes he killed Jen, but he was angry. It was a fit of rage—"

"Sweetheart, he killed his girlfriend, had a plan to explain her murder, then made up a new plan to blame you once you ruined his cover. All that points to a guy used to walking on the wrong side of the law and using his badge to cover his ass."

She nodded in agreement. "I suppose you're right."

"Can you think of any way to prove David killed Jen? Evidence of some kind? Fingerprints, DNA?"

She shook her head. "He came over a lot. His fingerprints would be all over the apartment. And I'm sure he tampered with any DNA evidence pointing to him. He told me that's what he would do."

Maybe they could somehow show David tampered with the evidence. It wouldn't prove guilt, but it would cast suspicions. Enough to open an investigation to Kayla's claims.

"I don't see how we are going to catch him."

Her weary voice tugged at his heart. Pulling her to him, he wrapped his arms around her, pressing his lips to her brow. "We *will* get him, Kayla. Make no mistake. David Tyler will face what he did to your friend." When he heard a sniffle, Ryder tipped his head down and placed a finger under her chin. "Hey, are you crying?"

Weeping women always got to him. His sister knew exactly how to get her way when they were younger. Julie just had to turn on the water works, and he would do whatever she wanted. An unhappy woman made his chest ache. He tried everything to make his mother smile in the months following his father's death. Some days it worked, others, he just held her while she cried.

"I don't understand you." Blue-green eyes stared at him in wonder. "You barely know me and yet, you're risking so much to help me. I'm not used to people being so kind."

He stared at her beautiful face. Eyes bright with tears. Full, succulent, lips trembling with emotion. She looked like a woman in need of a long, hard night of lovemaking. He wanted to kiss those tears away. Devour that mouth until the only worry in her head was how far away the bed was. He wanted to strip her naked and worship every inch of her delectable body.

Bet she wouldn't think of him as kind if she knew those thoughts were running through his mind right now.

"Well…" He cleared his throat, trying to dislodge the image of a naked, well-spent Kayla from his mind. *Not much luck with that, buddy.* "Then you must know some pretty crappy people."

She grimaced. "Yeah, I do."

"Come on. Let's go watch some mind-melting TV." He let her go, missing the warmth of her touch immediately, but knowing if he held her for much longer he was going to lose control. The woman tested his libido like no one else, and she wasn't even trying. "You need a break from all this."

She laughed softly, dabbing at her eyes with the sleeve of her sweater. "I so do."

They sat on the small loveseat in the living room. Ryder flipped through the channels until he found a classic comedy from the early nineties. He loved this movie; it always made him laugh. Hopefully, it would do the same for Kayla.

It was almost to the part where the uncle made a giant pancake for the little boy's birthday when Kayla snuggled into his side. He grabbed the afghan from the back of the couch, laying it over her. She smiled up at him, then turned her attention back to the television. A warm, comforting sensation filled his chest. This felt so right, so natural. Sitting here with her, relaxing, watching TV as if they had done this a million times.

His gut clenched with the realization he could do this a million more.

Chapter 12

"Oh no, Jen! Wake up, please!"

Hot tears fell onto her hands, mixing with the blood. She could cry for a thousand years and not have enough tears to wash away all that red. Dark, thick, and in the wrong place. It was all over the floor. It was supposed to be in Jen's body, giving her life. Why was it all over the floor?

Kayla shook her best friend, willing Jen with every fiber of her being to wake up. It did no good. Jen wasn't waking up. Not ever.

No! What was she going to do without her?

"Please don't go. I need you."

Who would eat cookie dough straight from the bowl with her? Who would go to bad horror movies with her just to laugh at the terrible plot line? Who would spend hours over a glass of red wine dissecting her latest crush?

Latest crush...

Something sparked in the back of her mind. There was someone she wanted to talk to Jen about, a man with long dark hair who rode a large, gray horse. A warrior of the law...

"You shouldn't be here."

The snarl came from behind her, and she whipped her head around to find David. Only he looked off, bigger than she remembered. Bigger and meaner. His eyes were black and soulless, like the lifeless eyes of a doll.

"You'll pay for killing Jen." His harsh voice seemed to come from everywhere, and yet his mouth never moved.

"I-I didn't kill her. I loved Jen." Tears she had no power over poured from her eyes until she was drowning in them. "David, please help me!"

His cruel lips curved in a demonic smile. "There's no help for you, Kayla. Why would anyone help a nothing like you? Mommy didn't love you, Daddy didn't love you, and Jen didn't love you, either. No one ever wanted you, and no one will ever love you."

He threw back his head and laughed, and the sound pierced her ears with the shock of a cannon boom. Screaming, she clasped her hand over her ears to block him out, but it did no good. The cruel laughter now came from inside her head.

"Stop it!" she bellowed into the clamor.

"Oh, I'll stop." David walked slowly toward her. "I'll make everything stop." Larger than life fingers wrapped around her throat and squeezed. "Forever."

Kayla gasped for breath. Clawing at David, she feebly smacked at him with her blood-covered hands. His laughter mocked as he pressed harder, and she struggled to suck in a breath. Her vocal chords constricted as she tried to scream.

He smiled gleefully, his eyes alight with madness. "Go ahead. No one will hear you."

She was dying. She knew that. Had Jen known she was dying? Had it felt like this, full of terror and regret? So many things she wanted to do in life, so many goals to accomplish. To have it end like this. It didn't seem right.

David's hands clenched tighter until her vision dimmed. In her fading sight, she saw her savior on his gray horse, and a name came to her.

"Ryder," she croaked, the word barely audible.

David ground his teeth together. "Die, bitch. Die!"

"Ryder," she called with more force.

David shook her, his rage growing like an ember in a fire.

No! She would not die this way. She had to live— for Jen. Someone had to let everyone know what really happened.

Sucking in a deep breath, Kayla kicked out her foot, connecting directly with her target, David's balls. He howled in pain, releasing her and grabbing the offended area. Kayla opened her mouth wide and screamed. "Ryder!"

"I've got you now, sweetheart. You're safe."

The deep, soothing voice called to her from the darkness.

"Come back to me now."

Strong, warm arms surround her. Not threatening like David's had been, but comforting, protective. Heart racing wildly, she breathed deep. Woods, musk, man. She knew that smell. She trusted that smell.

"Ryder?" Kayla opened her tear-filled eyes.

His concerned face peered down at her. "Yeah, honey. It's me." Dark brown eyes gazed at her with apprehension. "You were screaming. Having a nightmare I think."

It came back to her—Jen in a pool of blood, David trying to kill her. She shuddered, and Ryder's arms tightened around her, offering security.

She threw hers around him, burying her face against his neck. "It was awful."

"David?"

The one word, all he needed to ask. She nodded.

He ran a hand up and down her back in a soothing gesture while whispering in her ear. "It's all right now. You're safe. I won't let him hurt you."

Humiliation started to creep in. For heaven's sake, she was a twenty-five year old woman. She shouldn't need comforting after a nightmare. "I'm sorry if I woke you."

"Sweetheart, you were screaming my name."

Oh, even better. Was there a hole somewhere she could hide in?

"Scared the life out of me to hear you scream like that." His grip on her was firm, but not painful. "I ran in here thinking that bastard had somehow found you."

He had. In her dreams. She could run as far as she wanted, but it appeared she would never outrun David Tyler. It had only been a nightmare, but she knew the man would never stop searching for her. Once he found her, he would eliminate her...and anyone helping her who could threaten his story.

"I should leave."

The stroking stopped. Ryder held himself perfectly still. "Leave?"

Pain sliced her heart at the thought of leaving, but it was the right thing to do. She couldn't allow Ryder to be hurt because of her. "It's dangerous for me to stay."

"I promise that sick bastard won't get anywhere near you, Kayla."

She pushed away, staring up into those tempting, chocolate brown eyes. Good grief, she wanted this man, more than she had ever wanted anything in her life. How could she not? He was kind, brave, sexy as sin. Every woman's dream. But she was living a nightmare. No way could she drag him into her problems.

"It's better if I go."

His eyes narrowed. "I thought we already had this discussion."

"It's not fair for me to bring my troubles to your door."

The corner of his mouth kicked up in a smug grin. "Bring them on, baby."

The man infuriated her. She was trying to do the right thing here, and he was being so stubborn.

"I don't want you getting hurt because of me."

The rough pads of his fingers gently brushed her damp cheek. Such a strong hand, but kind and gentle. So unlike David's in her dream.

"It was a nightmare, honey. Don't worry about me. I'm tougher than I look."

He looked plenty tough to her.

She let her gaze roam over his body and realized Ryder only wore a loose pair of pajama bottoms. His chest was bare, and now she couldn't seem to focus on anything else. Gaze glued to him, she took in every plane and dip, every muscle and contour. The man was a well-honed machine. A light dusting of hair trailed from his chest down a set of scrumptious looking abdominal muscles and disappeared underneath the waistband of his pants.

A flush crept up her chest as the temperature in the bedroom became very hot.

"Kayla." His deep voice brought her attention back to his face. "Are you okay now? Do you think you'll be able to sleep?"

What? Sleep? What were we talking about? Her mind had gone suddenly blank, wiped out by the vision of Ryder's naked torso.

"You're not scared anymore?" His brows drew down in worry.

Scared? Oh right, her nightmare. David trying to kill her. It all came back with horrifying clarity. She shivered, and Ryder took note, his arm coming around her again.

"Would you like me to stay for a bit?"

She wanted to say no, wanted to be strong, but she knew, left alone, she wouldn't get back to sleep. Meekly, she nodded. "Would you mind sleeping with me tonight?"

Heat flooded her face as her own words sank in. Oh goodness, did she really just proposition him? How pathetic could she get? "I didn't mean—I only meant that, um, I—"

He chuckled at her self-conscious struggle. "I know what you meant, honey. Of course I'll stay with you tonight." His eyes twinkled with humor. "For sleeping. Nothing more."

Ready to save David the hassle of killing her and just die of embarrassment right then and there, she turned on her side so her back faced Ryder. She held herself stiff until his arm came around her. His body heat radiated through her as he pressed himself flush against her. She couldn't stop herself from snuggling back against the warm security he offered.

He kissed her neck softly, right below her ear, whispering in the darkness, "Goodnight, sweetheart."

The gentle care he offered brought moisture to her

eyes. Her racing heart calmed, nerves settled by the presence of being held in Ryder's strong arms. This time when she closed her eyes, instead of fear and darkness, there was only calm and peace.

Chapter 13

"I found something you're going to want to take a look at."

At Jim Foster's words, David glanced up. His partner sat on the edge of his desk, a thumb drive in his hand.

"What is it?"

"Security footage from a bus station in bumfuck Kansas." He chuckled at the mention of anyone wanting to visit Kansas.

David reached for the drive, plugging it into his computer.

"There's our girl." Foster pointed to the screen as the video played.

He stared. Sure enough, there, in the middle of the bus terminal, stood Kayla Jenkins. So, she ditched her car. Smart girl. He'd had an APB out on her plates minutes after she fled the scene, and wondered why no one had spotted it yet. She probably stashed it somewhere.

Bitch is smart.

But he was smarter.

He watched the screen. Kayla glanced up, her attention rapt on something in the corner. A television no doubt. Had she seen the press conference? Did she watch as he called her out to the world as a murderer? She must have, because after a moment of focus, she started to dart her head around.

That's right, honey. Be afraid. I will find you, and I will kill you.

He watched as she hunched in on herself, trying to hide. It didn't matter. No one paid her any attention. She turned and quickly headed out of the bus station. The feed cut off, and David was left staring at his own tense reflection in the black screen.

"That's it?"

Foster's smug grin faltered. "Well, yeah. We got her on tape. We know where she is."

Idiot. He chose to work with Jim because he knew he could bribe the other man if the time came, but Foster didn't have the good sense God gave a rat.

"No." He clenched his teeth so he didn't go off on the guy. "We know where she *was.* Surely, you don't think she stayed in Kansas?"

The cop stared at him with a blank expression, as if, yes, he did think she stayed right where she was.

Grade A moron.

"Where did she go after she left the bus terminal?"

His temporary partner shrugged. "Hell, I don't know. They only sent us this. One of their security guys noticed it when he reviewed the tapes."

"Did you ask for any additional footage? Check to see if they had outside cameras?"

At least the guy had the decency to look contrite. It was shoddy police work. Not that he wanted stellar work on this case. If people did their jobs well enough they'd see the holes, and one thing after another would add up, equaling him. He couldn't let that happen. That was why he needed to find Kayla, kill her, and give everyone the ending to this tragic story all wrapped up in a nice, neat, little bow.

But to do that, he needed to know where the hell she was!

Glaring at his partner, he tried to keep his voice calm. "So, you bring me this video that's days old judging from the time stamp and expect me to jump for joy because we know where Kayla was seventy-two hours ago?" The rage built inside of him. To maintain his story, he added an emotional crack to his voice. "This woman killed my girl, Jim. I need to find her."

The man rubbed the back of his neck, clearly uncomfortable with the emotions David falsified. "I'm sorry, man. I know this is tough for you. Let me call the bus station back. I'll speak to the guy in charge, see if they have anything more."

He shook his head. "Forget it. I think it would be better if I went down there myself. Checked it out in person."

"Sounds good. Let me grab my coat."

He waved a hand in the air. "No. I'll take this one solo."

Foster hesitated. "I don't think the chief would—"

"You let me deal with the chief. Besides, I want you to go check out a lead in Vegas. Kayla had a foster family there she really connected with when she was younger. She might have run back to them."

Total bullshit. There was no foster family in Vegas. He just needed Jim out of his hair, distracted for a few days. What better place to distract a man than Sin City?

"Vegas?" The guy sounded skeptical.

Time to dangle the carrot.

Reaching into his desk, he grabbed the white envelope stuffed with cash he'd placed there the day

Chief Vic said he needed a partner. Slipping it into a file folder, he handed it over. "Yeah, Vegas. Think about this. If the lead turns up to be a wild goose chase, you can always take a day or two of personal time." He indicated the folder with a raise of his brow. "You know, a little R and R."

Foster glanced around with a slight turn of his head. Opening the folder, he reached in and thumbed through the envelope. When he looked back up, his greedy eyes gleamed with understanding. "Looks like I'm off to Sin City."

The perfect place for a guy like him.

"I'll let you know if I…find anything."

Good, Foster was on board. He probably thought David was paying him off so he could go after Kayla himself. Complete the revenge killing the chief warned him against. Didn't matter what the other man thought. Jim Foster would be out of the way now, and that was all that mattered.

David left the police station and got into his big, black SUV, a birthday gift from his father. He drove straight to his apartment, grabbed some clothes and his laptop, and was back on the road in less than thirty minutes.

It took the whole damn day to drive to Kansas. One long, boring drive where he let his mind wander to all the ways he could kill Kayla once he found her. It had to look like an accident—an accident he tried to save her from. No matter what, he had to look like the good guy, the hero. There could be no doubt cast upon him. A car accident while running from the cops or a self-inflicted gunshot would work.

That last one sounded plausible. Suspects turned

the gun on themselves all the time. Facing prison was a scary thing, some people couldn't handle it. They opted for the easy way out—suicide. Yeah, he could make that happen. If that didn't work, he could always say there was a struggle. Kayla got killed when going for his gun.

He could make that story fly, too. After all, everyone already believed him about Jen's murder.

Darkness settled over the flat landscape outside the car. David flicked his headlights on and consulted his GPS. Five more miles. He glanced to the side, taking in the scenery. Or, really, lack thereof. Foster had been right, this place was bumfuck USA. No buildings or trees, just flat, empty fields.

He took a sip of the cold coffee he bought two hours ago during his last gas fill up. It tasted like shit, but he needed the caffeine. Up ahead, he saw a scattering of lights in the distance.

Welcome to bland town, he thought with a grimace.

Not soon enough, he pulled into the parking lot of the bus station and killed his engine. The sun had set long ago, casting the road in darkness. The bright, fluorescent lights outside the bus terminal blinded him as he got out of his car and headed for the building. Once inside, he identified the security office and headed straight for it. A middle-aged man whose gut hung over his uniform belt sat at the desk, playing on his phone and completely ignoring the security monitors. David cleared his throat, but the man's focus was firmly on his phone.

"Excuse me?"

"Ticket booth is over there," fatty said with a nod of his head.

The guy's thumbs rapidly moved over the small screen. Texting or playing a game, David didn't care. In no mood after driving over ten hours, he slammed his badge down on the counter. Fatty jumped in surprise, dropping his captivating phone.

"Chicago PD." That got his attention. "Someone from here sent us a tape from a few days ago."

"A t-t-tape?"

The man stuttered like an idiot. He seemed to be surrounded by them lately.

"A *security* tape. There was a woman on the footage. She was at this station approximately three days ago. She's wanted for murder."

Fatty's eyes widened. "Oh, right. Let me check on that for you, sir."

The pathetic excuse for a security guard fumbled though some paperwork on his desk as he waited with rapidly waning patience.

"Here it is." The guy held up a memo triumphantly. "Yeah, it looks like one of our guys was reviewing tapes to catch the person who's been vandalizing our soda machine."

He could give a flying fuck about their soda machine.

"He found the video of your suspect and sent it your way."

Fatty beamed at him as if he had just given David the secret to eternal life. Dumbass hadn't told him anything he didn't already know.

"Did anyone happen to know where she went *after* she left the station? Do you have outside cameras?"

The chubby head shook.

He couldn't keep his growl of frustration quiet. The

guard jumped at the sound. Big guy was so easily startled. How the hell did he get into security work?

"Um, we don't have any cameras outside the terminal, but the drug store down the street has outside cameras. Maybe they caught a shot of your suspect."

Without a parting word, David turned and headed out of the terminal in search of the drug store. He could see the lights from the parking lot so left his car at the bus station. He needed the walk to let off steam anyway.

As he wrenched opened the drug store door, he noticed they did indeed have outside cameras, inside ones as well.

An electronic bing alerted the cashier to his presence. A young, skinny male, the kid couldn't have been more than twenty with an acne pocked face and big, wide eyes that grew wider as David approached the counter.

"Can I help you, sir?"

At least this worker seemed to know what a goddamn job meant. "I'm Officer David Tyler of the Chicago PD." He flashed his badge. "I need to see your outside security footage from three days ago."

The employee leaned around him to yell at someone in the back of the store. "Mr. Garret, there's a police officer here. He needs our camera footage."

David turned to see a man, probably in his late fifties—judging from the graying hair at his temples—coming up an aisle toward him.

"Officer David Tyler, Chicago PD." He showed his badge to the older man.

"Bruce Garret, manager and owner." He sniffed, rubbing a finger across the bushy moustache that hung over his top lip. "You need to see our security footage?"

"Yes. There was a woman at the bus station the other night. She's wanted for murder. Their footage showed her leaving the station, but they have no outside cameras. I was hoping to check out your footage. She might have walked by your shop. It would give us a lead on where she went next."

"You say she's a murderer?"

"Killed in cold blood."

Garret turned, waving for him to follow. "Come on back. We'll check it out. I'll be in back with the officer, Evan," the owner called to the pocked-faced teen.

"Yes, sir."

They wound their way through the aisles, passing through a door marked *Employees Only*. Garret offered him a seat in front of an old computer that looked like it had seen better days.

"What day did you say she was in town?"

"Three days ago."

The older man started to cue up the footage.

"I hate to trouble you further, but I've been driving all day. Could I get a cup of coffee?"

He needed the caffeine fix, but he also needed to watch the tape alone.

"Sure." Garret finished clicking at the computer and rose. "Need something to eat, too? I ordered a pizza for the staff today. Think there's still some left."

"That'd be great, thanks."

"No problem, officer."

What a good Samaritan. David smiled to himself as the old man left the room. Being a cop had perks, and he knew how to use every single one of them.

Once Garret was gone, he clicked to the file of the day he needed and started running through the tape. Four views split the computer screen, one outside and three inside the store. It wasn't long before he spotted Kayla hurrying along the sidewalk.

Bingo!

His lips curled in triumph as he watched her entered the store. *Even better.* He shifted his attention from screen to screen as he followed her movements. She made her way down the aisles, picking up things as she went. He observed as she grabbed a T-shirt, a box of hair dye, and a pair of scissors. Then, she went to the front, paid for them, and left the store.

The bitch thought to change her appearance? *Shit.* She was making this harder for him. With the way she anticipated things, it almost felt like she had experience running from the cops. He knew she didn't. Kayla was annoyingly lawful. Must be all those stupid crime shows she watched with Jen. Hollywood didn't know dick about real police work. Those shows were a joke.

So, she colored and cut her hair. Didn't matter. He'd still find her.

"Here you go, officer." Garret returned with coffee and a plate piled with three pieces of pepperoni pizza in hand. "You find what you were looking for?"

He stood, blocking the older man's view of the computer while pressing the keys to delete the footage.

"No. Unfortunately, it looks like your footage of that day is missing."

Bushy gray brows drew together. "Damn, again? I'm sorry, Officer Tyler. Our system is older than dirt, and it gets bugs from time to time. There's not much crime here. I really only use it as a deterrent."

The guy was actually buying it *and* apologizing. Everyone in this town was dumb as shit.

"I'm sorry I couldn't help."

He accepted the coffee and pizza with a smile. "Not to worry." Suppressing a gleeful chuckle, he took a small sip. "You've been very, *very* helpful."

Kayla might be on the run, but he was closing in on her. Soon, she would no longer be a problem.

Chapter 14

The smell woke Ryder—the sweet smell of warm femininity. He leaned his head down, brushing his nose against the crown of Kayla's head, enjoying the fragrance unique to her. It was strange, since she had been staying here with him she'd been using the guest bathroom stocked full of his sister's products. Ergo, she should smell like Julie, but she didn't.

The lilac shampoo smelled distinctly different on her. The lavender body wash conjured up images in his head of Kayla lying in a field of wildflowers, completely naked. Ready and waiting for him. Definitely *not* the same thoughts that came to mind around his sister.

And it was an odd experience waking up with his arms around a woman. He didn't date much. In his youth, he'd been too busy trying to take care of his mother and sister. Now, he was so wrapped up in his job taking care of the town, he never had much time for more than a quick release. Staying the night with a lover rarely happened. There had never been anyone he cared enough about to make the time.

Until now.

He opened his eyes. Kayla lay on his chest, out like a light. Her hair was a mess of soft tangles. The silky strands tickled his bare skin. Her arms were loosely wrapped around his neck, clutching him like a lifeline, even in her sleep. With one leg draped over his hips, her entire body was plastered tight to his side. Incredible.

This brave, beautiful, strong woman, who had well-reasoned trust issues, was completely relaxed in his arms. She'd been through hell, had every right to keep on running, but she didn't. She'd put her faith in him, in the assurance that he could help her. It humbled and terrified him. He could not let her down.

She let out a soft moan in her sleep, a sexy little sound causing him to examine their position once more. With him in pajama pants and Kayla in nothing but a thin nightshirt, his body quickly realized the opportunity this situation presented. Much as he would love to take advantage of said situation, he knew she was still too vulnerable. Sex would be amazing and a great distraction, but he didn't want to be her distraction. When they got together—and they would— he wanted it to be because she wanted *him*.

Unfortunately, his brain forgot to tell his body that little moral tidbit. His mind wasn't the only thing awake and alert. There was a pup tent situation happening that would get real embarrassing for both of them if she woke up and moved her knee about two inches north.

Carefully, so as not to wake her, he shifted her off of him and onto her back. Her mouth opened wide in a jaw-cracking yawn.

"Morning, sweetheart."

Her eyes shot open. She looked like a deer caught in the headlights of a car. It was so cute he wanted to laugh. Instead, he bent down and brushed a kiss on her forehead.

"Did you sleep well?"

Lips pressed together firmly, she nodded.

"No more nightmares?"

Mouth still closed tight, she shook her head.

"Good." He toyed with a strand of her hair. "Up for some breakfast?"

Again she nodded, not speaking. A sinking feeling settled in his gut. Had he made her uncomfortable by staying all night? Should he have left before she woke? Was she upset with him, embarrassed? He stayed because she asked him to. Also, secretly, because he needed to hold her.

Never one to shy away from a problem, he went for the direct approach. "Kayla? What's wrong?"

She shook her head, trying to hide under the covers.

Like hell.

She couldn't ask him to comfort her, trust him with her secret and pain, and then hide from him. He wouldn't push her sexually, but she didn't get to retreat emotionally.

"Sweetheart, what is it?" Tugging on the quilt, he asked the question he feared, "Are you upset that we slept together? Nothing happened, you know that right? I would never force you to do anything you didn't want to do."

She nodded, rolling her eyes at him like he was crazy for saying that. The knot in his stomach loosened. Okay, so she wasn't upset because he held her all night. Then what was it?

"Come on, talk to me."

Scowl firmly in place, she gave a resigned sigh. Holding a hand over her mouth, she mumbled, "I just woke up."

He stared in confusion. "I know."

Her beautiful hazel eyes rolled again with annoyance. "I haven't gotten a chance to brush my teeth, and I didn't want to gross you out."

Relief flooded him. Women, they thought a little thing like morning breath would put a guy off. Shoot, half the time his breath smelled like onions and feet. Never embarrassed him much, but he could see how it would bother someone as polite and sweet as Kayla.

Gently pulling her hand away from her mouth, he bent his head down. Ever so slightly, he brushed his lips over hers. He didn't want to rush her, but he knew he couldn't last another minute without tasting her. He kept it brief. If he didn't, he risked losing control, and that was the last thing she needed.

"Nothing you could ever do would gross me out, sweetheart. Trust me." He pulled back and saw the shock in her eyes. There was something else there…heat. She wanted him, too. Not enough though, not yet.

"I've helped castrate a bull before. Once you do that, a little morning breath is nothing. Besides, I just woke up myself. I'm sure my breath could knock out a Clydesdale at fifty paces."

She laughed. "Have you really castrated a bull?"

A shudder passed through his body at the memory. "Yup. This is ranching country, and the sheriff has to help out whenever necessary. It was an experience I hope I never have to repeat."

She smiled, and the beauty of this woman, once again, struck him. An inner glow seemed to shine from every pore of her being. Shit, she was turning him into a freaking poet.

"I have to go into work today."

Her breathing hitched, and fear entered her gaze. He hated seeing that; it cut like a blade to the chest.

"I don't want you staying here alone, just in case David picks up on your trail." And also because he didn't want her getting scared again and running, but he kept that part to himself.

"I was thinking it might be fun for you to spend the day at the Denning ranch. You remember Lizzy, the woman we ran into the other day?"

She nodded, expression blank.

"Well, she and her business partner live on a ranch with their fiancés."

"The brothers?"

"Yeah. What do you think?"

She worried her bottom lip. Ryder had the urge to dip his head and capture that poor, bruised lip with his mouth, soothe the worry with his tongue, but he'd already set her off guard enough for one morning. Keeping his thirst in control around this woman was getting harder and harder. She tempted him like no other.

"Sure," she said after a moment of thought. "That sounds like it could be fun."

He grinned at her abysmal attempt to look enthusiastic.

"I know Lizzy can be a bit…much. But she's great, and so is Maggie. The guys are real stand up, too. Plus, they have a whole mess of ranch hands. You'll be safe. I promise."

She nodded, but the worry still shone plain on her face.

"I better let you get dressed."

At the mention of clothes, or lack thereof, she blushed. Ryder chuckled, rising from the bed, unashamed of his partial nudity. Thankfully, his body had calmed down enough that "little Ryder" wasn't making himself obvious anymore.

"I need to check on Wind Chaser, then I'll make us a quick breakfast. Then we'll head out."

Kayla nodded, but her gaze was wide and glued to his chest. His pride puffed up at her look of unmasked desire. Perhaps she wanted him more than he thought.

"Give me about thirty minutes, okay?"

She shook her head, mutely, her gaze still eating up his naked flesh. Shit, if he didn't leave soon that heated stare of hers was going to make him forget his promise to take things slow. There was a spark, hell, damn near fire, but he didn't want to rush anything. The whole situation was a muddled mess at the moment. They needed time to sort through everything and make sure they were both on the same page. Now was not the right time...but soon, very soon.

Quickly, before things got even *harder*, he stepped out of the room and into his to change. After seeing to Wind Chaser's morning needs, he took a quick—and very cold—shower, and set out a breakfast of hot oatmeal and toast.

Kayla—dressed in a pair of her new jeans and a green sweater that set off her eyes perfectly—joined him at the table. They ate in silence. It was strange, but not uncomfortable. In fact, the whole experience felt quite pleasant.

He helped her bundled up against the cold, and they got in his truck.

The Denning ranch was on the outskirts of town,

like his own place, so Ryder didn't need to drive into town to get to the ranch. Thankfully, the roads were clear, and it only took about ten minutes to get there.

He pulled the truck up into the driveway, spotting Colton and Dade immediately. They noticed him right off and walked toward the truck as he turned off the engine.

Kayla twisted her hands nervously.

Reaching across the seat, he pried her fingers apart, taking them in his own and gently squeezing. "Hey, it's going to be okay. These are good guys. I promise."

"Yeah?" She bit her lip; poor thing would be bruised from all the abuse she gave it.

"Trust them with my life." More importantly, he trusted them with hers.

She took a deep breath, letting it out with a firm nod of her head. "Okay."

He knew this was hard for her, trusting men she didn't know with her safety. It had to be hard to trust people given what she had gone through in less than a week. Damn, she was an amazing woman. Every moment they spent together, his admiration for her grew.

"Hey, Sheriff." Colton Denning grinned as he approached, grasping his hand in a quick shake as Ryder left the truck. "What brings you to our neck of the woods? Did my brother forget to pay a parking ticket again?"

"Shut up, Colt. That was one time." Dade shoved his brother slightly.

"Lock him up, Sheriff. We can't have these delinquents running around ruining our town's good name."

Dade rolled his eyes at his younger brother's antics. "Hey, Ryder. What can we do for you?"

Used to the brothers' playful banter, he moved around the side of the truck. "Guys, I want you to meet my friend Kayla. Kayla, this is Colton and Dade Denning."

Colton's face lit up with recognition. "Oh yeah. Lizzy was telling us about you the other night. She met you in town?"

She pressed herself to his side meekly. "Yes, she was very…nice."

Dade, who had been studying her with an intense stare, laughed loudly. "You mean pushy and nosy. I know my fiancée. She can be a bit overwhelming when you first meet her, but she grows on you."

"I'm telling her you said that." The younger Denning nudged his brother.

"You do and I'll tell Maggie what you said last week about the new rug."

Colton clutched his chest in horror. "You wouldn't dare!"

"Try me."

The cowboy threw a beseeching glance to Kayla. "Betrayed by my own brother, can you believe the nerve of this guy? Besides, it's not my fault my future wife has terrible taste in rugs."

"Now we all heard you say it."

"You heard nothing." Colton sent a mock glare around the group.

Ryder chuckled, noting with relief the nervous tension recede from Kayla's body as the brothers charmed her.

"You folks eaten yet?" Dade asked, ignoring his

brother. "We just finished breakfast, but I'm sure Maggie can fix you up something."

He shook his head. "We've already eaten, thanks. Kayla, why don't you go into the house and let Lizzy introduce you to Maggie while I talk to the guys?"

She hesitated, glancing at the brothers.

Colton smiled. "Go on in. I know my fiancée is dying to meet you."

With a shaky smile, she headed toward the house.

Once she was inside, the door firmly shut behind her, Dade spoke. "So, Ryder." He crossed his arms over his chest. "I assume you came out here for more than an introduction?"

He removed his hat from his head, running a hand through his long hair. He hadn't had a chance to braid it for work yet.

"I can't explain everything," he started as the brothers stared at him with worried expressions in their identical blue eyes. "Kayla is in some trouble. She's got a guy after her. A real bad guy."

Dade's jaw tightened; Colton's smile vanished. They both had recent experience with threats poised against their women and would understood his caution. Not that Kayla was his woman. Not yet, anyway.

"He doesn't know where she is for now, but that might change."

"You got a name for this asshole?" Colton asked.

"David Tyler. He's a cop from Chicago."

"Shit, a bad cop?" Dade swore.

He nodded. "I don't want to leave her all alone at my place when I'm working. I know it's an imposition, but could she spend the day here?"

Colton stared at him as if he was crazy. "You really

need to ask, man? After all you've done for this town, all you've done for us? For Maggie and Lizzy? Of course she can stay here."

"We'll keep your woman safe, Ryder. That's a promise," Dade said in his calm manner.

"Thanks, guys. I really appreciate it. I better go say goodbye before I leave."

Colton grinned. "The women will be please as mares in mating season that you finally found someone. They've been planning on pimping you out at the wedding, trying to hook you up with a lady."

He shook his head. "It's not like that." *Yet.* "I'm just helping out a friend."

The brothers shared a glance saying he was kidding himself. Maybe, but they didn't know the whole story.

Yes, he wanted Kayla. Wanted her with a bone-deep hunger that grew with every second of the day. But she wasn't ready. Right now, she needed him to help her, not hump her. Until he knew she was ready, he had to keep his hands to himself.

He thought of last night, holding her while she slept, kissing her softly that morning…

Okay, mostly to himself. He wasn't a saint after all.

The loud peals of laughter reached his ears as he entered the house through the kitchen door. The three women were sitting at the table, Maggie and Kayla drinking coffee while Lizzy held a mug of steaming peppermint tea by the smell of it.

"Hello, ladies."

They glanced up. Kayla smiled brightly at him; Maggie and Lizzy shared a knowing grin behind her.

"I'm going to head into work now," he spoke to Kayla. "You gonna be okay?"

She nodded with a smile. "Lizzy was telling me about the time she tried to make s'mores and burned her eyebrows off."

"I had to draw them on." Strawberry blonde curls bounced as she explained. "It was hilarious. I looked surprised for an entire month."

The women broke into giggles again.

Ryder smiled, knowing Kayla was well in hand. "I'll be back around six, okay?"

She nodded, and Maggie spoke up. "You can both stay for dinner." One eyebrow rose as she eyed him. "You owe us a dinner visit anyway, Ryder."

He chuckled, knowing full well Maggie was using this as an excuse to determine the nature of his and Kayla's relationship. Poor Kayla, she'd have to field questions all day. Still, better than staying home alone in his empty house worrying about David.

"That I do, Maggie. All right then, see you at six for dinner."

He tipped his hat to the women and headed out the door. Before it shut behind him, he heard a chair scrape. There was a tug on his arm, and he turned to see Kayla standing there.

She threw her arms around him, hugging him tight. "Thank you, Ryder," she whispered softly against his neck. "For everything."

She pulled back, and he saw something in her eyes. Gratitude, hope, and if he wasn't mistaken, desire. The last one sucker punched him. She was making it damn hard for him to be noble.

He stroked a finger down the softness of her cheek. "Call me if you need anything. Everyone here has my number."

Her head bobbed in agreement. Then, surprising the hell out of him, she rose up on her toes and pressed her lips firmly against his. His shock only lasted a moment before he closed his eyes to savor the kiss. Her sweet little tongue rasped against the seam of his lips, and he opened willingly for her. They had a captive audience so he kept it light, brushing his tongue softly against hers. Tasting her when what he really wanted to do was devour. It was heavenly, blistering, and over too soon.

He pulled back, reluctantly, both of their breathing unsteady. Kayla's entire face was flushed, the look of a woman needy and ready for more. Damn fine time for her to let him know.

"I'll see you later." His voice came out harsh with unsated need.

Ignoring the high-five Lizzy gave Maggie behind them, he turned and headed back out into the cold. The wind stirred, blowing snow from the ground into his face, but he didn't feel it. After that scorching hot kiss from Kayla, he felt like he was in the freaking tropics. Damn, if she got him that hot over one little kiss, he wondered what was going to happen when they finally made love.

He got in his truck and drove to the station, wondering if he should put the fire extinguisher near his bed tonight.

Chapter 15

Kayla couldn't believe she just did that.

She'd meant it to be a light, friendly, thank-you kiss. The moment her lips touched Ryder's, though, all friendly thoughts had flown right out the window. It was like her mouth had a mind of its own, and that mind wanted Ryder.

Oh, who was she kidding? *She* wanted Ryder, mind, body, and soul. The man was a powder keg of sexual dynamite wrapped in helpful kindness. The dual assault on her emotions and her hormones was too much to endure. Jake Ryder was one amazingly special man.

So she kissed him and let the moment get away from her, who cared? It had been an amazing kiss full of passion and heat. She'd forgotten everything but the feel of his mouth. The man knew how to kiss. It made her wonder what else he knew how to do. Her face warmed as vivid, carnal scenes played out in her mind.

The clearing of a throat caused her to turn. Her face heated even more with embarrassment as she remembered she wasn't alone in the kitchen. There at the table, Lizzy and Maggie sat with identical expressions of smug satisfaction on their faces.

"Sooooo," Maggie began. "You and Ryder are…?"

"Friends," she answered quickly.

Just because she had strong feelings didn't mean he

did. Sure, he said they had a connection, but that didn't mean a romantic connection. And yes, he slept with her last night, but the key word was *slept*. Ryder had been a perfect gentleman through the entire night. He never once came onto her or pressured her. Yes, he touched her and kissed her softly every now and then, but they were caresses one might give a close friend or family member. He never once initiated intimate contact like she had only a moment ago.

Doubt began to sink in. What if Ryder just kissed her back to be polite? He *was* the kind of man who wouldn't reject a woman in front of others so as to spare her feelings. Oh no, she'd thrown herself on Ryder like a desperate hussy. Talk about embarrassing. After that display, he was probably high-tailing it to work, thankful to get away from the crazy woman. Probably thought she had some hero worship thing going on.

"Friends?" Lizzy scoffed. "No, honey. Ryder and *I* are friends. And if I kissed my friends the way you kissed Ryder, Dade would be cancelling our wedding before I could clean the spit off my lips."

Body flushing down to her toes, she returned to her seat at the table. "It's nothing, really."

"Yeah, and I'm not beginning to resemble the Pillsbury Dough Boy." Lizzy snorted out a laugh.

Maggie placed a hand on the other woman's arm. "Sweetie, you look beautiful."

She did. Kayla marveled at the expectant mother's ability to look like one of those pregnant women you see in fashion shoots. Lizzy's hair was a beautiful strawberry blonde, her makeup applied perfectly, and her clothing stylish while accentuating her growing bump.

"Thank you, Maggie. Dade keeps telling me the same thing. It's just weird watching my body change. Things keep getting bigger and bigger. I swear my ass has grown two sizes. I had to buy new underwear! How come none of the pregnancy books mention *that*?" Rubbing a hand over her belly, the mother-to-be smiled. "Still, it's pretty wonderzing."

Maggie shook her head with a smile. "That's not a word."

"It should be. Wonderful and amazing. It describes pregnancy perfectly." Lizzy wrinkled her nose in thought. "If you don't count all the nausea and heartburn."

Watching the two close women interact was comforting and heartbreaking at the same time. It reminded Kayla of her and Jen. They'd been so close. Some nights they would stay up for hours talking about their hopes and dreams. Over the years, they shared heartbreak, joy, and every aspect of their lives with each other. Now, she suddenly had no one; she still couldn't believe Jen was gone.

And I'm being blamed for it.

"Enough about my ever expanding waistline. We were discussing Kayla and Ryder."

"Yes," Maggie turned to face her. "So, exactly how *friendly* are you and our sheriff?"

"And by friendly, she means have you doinked him yet?"

"Lizzy! That is *not* what I meant, and who over the age of twelve says doinked?"

The beautiful blonde shrugged, taking a sip of her tea.

Kayla pulled herself out of her dark thoughts to respond. "It's not like that, really." The two other women shared a knowing glance, and she continued quickly, "He's helping me with some…trouble I'm having."

She watched as their sunny smiles disappeared. Maggie leaned toward her, placing a hand on her arm like she had done moments ago with Lizzy. The gesture was so sweet, it brought a tear to her eye. Damn, she missed her best friend. These two were so kind. Jen would have liked them.

"Is someone trying to hurt you?"

She couldn't help her eyes widening in shock at the correct assumption.

Lizzy smiled sadly. "Ryder helped Maggie and me out with some trouble we were having. Trouble being people who wanted to make us disappear."

"As sheriff, that's his job, but Ryder goes above and beyond the call of duty when it comes to protecting the people he cares about," the smaller woman added with a squeeze to her hand.

"He barely knows me." The soft confession slipped out.

"That may be true, but the way he looks at you…" Lizzy reached out, grasping her other hand. "There's something there. We can tell."

She hoped they were right. These feelings she had for Ryder kept growing and growing. It would be crushing if they were all one sided.

Then again, stupid to even be thinking of starting a romance with all that was going on in her life right now. She was on the run, being framed for murder for goodness sake. That kind of life did not lead to happily ever after and white picket fences.

Feeling confused and out of her element, she forced a smile at the women, pulling her hands away to grasp her coffee cup. Maggie and Lizzy smiled back, but didn't press for more. Sipping deeply from her coffee, grateful the women were letting the matter drop, she decided to change the subject. "So, tell me more about your dual wedding. Is it hard to agree on things?"

The women shared a glance she could not decipher.

"We may be best friends, but our tastes tend to run in opposite directions." Maggie laughed around a grimace.

Kayla sat, enjoying her coffee while listening to the two bantered back and forth, amiably, about their upcoming wedding. They joked about fashion and taste in décor. The menu being the one thing they seemed to agree on. Both women loved food. It made sense, seeing as how they owned a bakery together.

"The men are being smart and letting us handle most of the planning," Maggie told her.

"Yep," Lizzy chimed in. "The only request Dade has is he be allowed to wear his cowboy boots. I told him that was fine as long as he wore them in the honeymoon suite." She smiled devilishly. "His boots and nothing else."

"Lizzy!"

"Save a horse, ride a cowboy. Am I right?" The feisty woman lifted her mug in a toast.

Her friend smiled indulgently, lifting her mug as well.

Caught up in the warm cheer of such wonderful friendship, Kayla found herself joining in. "Yeehaw," she cheered along with them, and they all clinked their mugs.

They talked a little more, discussing the wedding, Lizzy's pregnancy, and the shop. For the first time in days, Kayla felt normal.

"Speaking of the shop..." Maggie glanced at the clock on the wall. "It's time to head into work."

"You want to come with us?" Lizzy asked, rising from the table. "It will be a lot more exciting than hanging out here. Cupcakes beat horse poop any day."

It would be nice to spend the day with these lovely women. They were so kind and friendly. Though the reminder of what she'd had with Jen made her a bit melancholy, they also gave her hope she might find some form of friendship again. "Sure, I'd like that."

"You're gonna like it even more once you taste Maggie's cupcakes. I think most of the baby weight I've gained has been in cupcake form."

She laughed, the lighthearted joking a welcome change from the stress and sadness taking over her life lately.

Maggie ran outside to tell Colton they were heading into town. The cupcake maker also said she would send Ryder a text, letting him know. At the reminder of why she was really here, some of Kayla's joy dissipated. She had to remember she wasn't really in town visiting Ryder like Maggie and Lizzy thought—she was on the run from a murderer who was trying to frame her and keep her quiet

A sinking feeling entered the pit of her stomach. If these women found out who she really was, why she was really staying with Ryder, would they still welcome her? Or would they turn her in? As much as she wanted to befriend these two lovely women, she had to stay vigilant. At the moment, she couldn't trust anyone but Ryder. And even then, she could trust the man with her safety…but could she trust him with her heart?

Chapter 16

"Hey, Sheriff?" the deputy yelled across the small police station.

"For pity's sake, Jason. Don't shout at the man. Walk the thirty feet to his desk and speak in a civilized tone," Mrs. Billings admonished.

The young man blushed, ducking his head like a school child being sent to the principal's office. Ryder felt a bit sorry for the kid. Mrs. Billings was a no-nonsense woman who believed in good manners and wasn't afraid to speak up when she felt the need. He may be the sheriff, but everyone knew she ran the office on a tight watch. Heck, the old lady even yelled at him a time or two. Mostly scolding him for his swearing. Which he tried not to do very often, but some cases caused a man to curse.

"Sorry, Mrs. Billings," Jason mumbled, keeping his head down as he navigated his way around her desk and through the room to Ryder.

He tried to wipe the smile from his face as the young deputy came to stand in front of him. No one liked to be yelled at by someone who reminded them of their sweet, little old grandma. No sense in kicking the kid while he was down.

"What is it, Jason?"

The skinny young man placed a stack of papers on his desk.

"These faxes came through for you. Also, I got a call from Len Miller. He says someone busted his fence again and some of his cows got loose." Jason shifted on his feet. "He was pretty upset about it. Seems to think some of the neighborhood kids did it as a prank. He wants us to round them all up and, his words not mine, 'throw them where the sun don't shine.'"

Ryder shuffled through the stack of papers with a sigh. Len Miller was the very definition of grumpy old man. The guy was a pain in his ass. He had a new complaint almost every week, and half of them revolved around the youth in this town and how out of control they were. His fence was old and broke with a strong gust of wind. Maybe the guys at the hardware store could donate some time and supplies to help build the old timer a new one. He made a note to check into it.

He glanced down at the faxes in his hands. A notice on this year's hunting permits and regulations from the Department of Wildlife. A winter storm advisory from the National Weather Service—*oh what a surprise, more snow headed our way*. A few local faxes from citizens reporting problems or concerns. Most called or emailed, but a few still faxed in their complaints.

Sifting through the papers, Ryder saw something that made his heart skip a beat. His pulse quickened and his mouth went dry. There in the middle of the stack was an APB from Chicago Illinois:

Wanted by the Illinois State Police: Kayla Marie Jenkins
Crime: Suspected Murder
Last Location Seen: Wilson Bus Terminal, Wilson

Kansas

Approximately five foot five inches, red hair, hazel eyes. Last seen wearing black slacks and a red winter coat. Anyone who thinks they have seen Ms. Jenkins or knows of her whereabouts please contact Officer David Tyler of the Chicago Police Department. Do not approach suspect as she is extremely dangerous and may be armed.

Underneath the transcript was a picture of Kayla. It took him a moment to recognize her because in the picture she had long, fiery red hair. He sucked in a breath, awestruck by the shiny copper strands cascading around her face and over her shoulders. The pounding of his heart drowned out every other noise in the station. Kayla had been right to cut and dye her hair, though he wanted to rage at the loss of something so beautiful, she would have been recognized in an instant with such memorable hair. She was smiling in front of a plain blue backdrop. It looked like a school photo, and he remembered she mentioned she was a kindergarten teacher.

Fear gripped him. The police were widening their search for Kayla. For the APB to reach Peak Town, it meant they were gunning full force for her. He glanced around the office. Jason and Tim were already gone. The young deputy had not mentioned the APB. Did that mean he didn't see it? Checking faxes was technically Ryder's job as sheriff, so it was safe to believe no one saw the picture claiming she was wanted for murder.

Carefully, he folded the paper and picked up his coat, draping it over his arm so he could covertly stuff the APB in the jacket pocket. No one but him had seen it, and it was going to stay that way. He was damned glad the fax came in today when he was at work. If he hadn't been there when it arrived, someone else might have seen it. With her dye and cut job, Kayla did look different, but it wouldn't take long for someone to recognize her from the wanted poster. Particularly if it was hanging in the police station day and night.

"I'm heading out for a bit. Call me if anything urgent comes in."

Mrs. Billings raised a brow, but nodded. He was sheriff; he didn't have to explain to anyone where he was going.

Ryder threw his coat on as he headed out of the office and into the cold winter air. Once he was inside his truck, alone, he pulled out his cell and placed a call.

The phone rang twice before a familiar, sweet voice came on the line.

"What do you want, butthead? I'm in the middle of something."

He chuckled at his sister's not so sweet response. "I need a favor."

"Sure big brother. Just so you know, this is like the tenth one this year. You owe me *so* big."

He rolled his eyes even though she couldn't see it over the phone. He loved his little sister, but she could be such a brat sometimes. "Yeah, yeah. I know."

"So, what's the favor?"

"I need you to check out the Chicago PD and see if they put an APB out on a Kayla Jenkins."

There was a pause on her end of the line.

"Does this have anything to do with that David Tyler guy you asked me to look into the other day?"

He'd called his sister asking her to check into the cop's files the day after Kayla confessed her situation to him. With Liam and Julie checking into the guy, one of them would hit on something. He hoped.

"Yes, it does."

"Are you in trouble, Jake?" Her voice trembled with worry.

Ah, damn. He never wanted to upset Julie. Since his father died, his entire goal in life had been to take care of her and make sure she never had to worry about anything, ever. Too bad his independent kid sister didn't make it easy on him.

"I'm fine, Julie, but someone I…care about might be in trouble. Can you just check for me?"

"Hold on."

He heard some clicking over the phone, the sound of fingers typing away on a keyboard.

After a moment, Julie came back on the line. "Okay, I see a local APB for her, but nothing that would have reached out as far as Colorado. What's the contact number?"

Ryder grabbed the paper from his pocket and read off the number on the bottom of the fax.

More clicking, then, "That's not the station's number, or their fax. Give me one more second."

Suspicion started to build as he waited for his sister to confirm what he'd already suspected.

"Okaaaaay," Julie drew the word out. "That number is the personal cell phone of one Mr. David Tyler."

Sonofabitch.

"It's not listed anywhere with the department, but I managed to do a reverse look up online and tracked it to Tyler."

The bastard was searching for Kayla under the

guise of the Chicago Police Department. He wanted to find her before anyone else did. That only meant one thing. A cold thread of unease climbed up Ryder's spine.

David Tyler wanted to kill Kayla.

The man didn't want her brought in alive. She could tell her side of the story. Officer Tyler couldn't allow that to happen. By the looks of this APB, he was aiming to find Kayla before his superiors…and take her out.

Over my dead body.

"Jake," his sister's soft voice spoke in his ear. "I haven't been able to find much on this Tyler guy, but what I did find isn't good."

"You found something?"

He heard a shuffling of papers on his sister's end.

"Yes. I managed to get a sealed record from when he was sixteen. It was expunged from his file since the crime was committed when he was underage." A low growl came over the line. "It shouldn't have been, but the guy has a very influential and rich family."

"Crime?" He gripped his phone so tight the plastic case cracked in his hand. "What did he do?"

Julie's sad sigh shot straight to his heart. "He beat up his girlfriend at the time."

Dammit!

He knew an act of rage like the one Kayla described couldn't have been a first time thing. Violence like that didn't just show up. It grew.

"What happened?" He was unable to keep the anger from his voice.

"It says a sixteen-year-old David Tyler got into an argument with his eighteen-year-old girlfriend at a party. They were both drinking and yelling, then the record states David hit his girlfriend in the face with an empty beer bottle. It broke her jaw and lacerated her cheek, requiring ten stitches."

"Why the hell isn't that bastard in jail?"

"It looks like he was sentenced to a hundred hours of community service and required to pay all the girl's medical bills."

"Which I'm sure his daddy paid."

"Yes," his sister agreed. "I would also hazard a guess his father also paid for the high-priced lawyer who brokered the deal. I've heard of this guy, and he's a rat. It's guys like him that give credence to all those stupid lawyer jokes."

Bad cops, bad lawyers, it really sucked when the people you were supposed to trust turned out to be scum.

"The lawyer, a Mr. Simms, used the fact that both teens were drinking as an excuse for David's behavior. He also said since the girl was eighteen and of legal age, David should be treated like the minor he was. He was, and I quote, 'too young to know the consequences of his actions.' Jeez, it looks like this guy pulled every trick in the book to get Tyler off."

"So, David Tyler assaults a woman, gets away with it, and then joins the police force years later? Unbelievable."

"The record was sealed since he was a minor at the time."

Minor or not, violence like that needed to be dealt with, not swept under the rug. His blood boiled thinking about people twisting the system to get away with crimes.

"Is this Kayla Jenkins the one you're trying to help? Did he hurt her, too?"

Yes, but not in the way his sister probably worried about. David Tyler hurt Kayla by taking away the most important person in the world to her. His violence had not disappeared; it'd just lain dormant. It wasn't the alcohol, or his age, it was the man. Ryder would be damned if he let David get away with it this time.

"Don't you worry about it, kiddo. I've got it all under control."

He heard his sister scoff. "I'll worry if I want to, old man."

"Email me that file, will you?"

"Already sent. And I'll keep digging. See what else I can find out about David 'Douchebag' Tyler."

He laughed at his sister's crude humor. "Thanks, but be careful, okay? This guy is bad news." The last thing he wanted was for Julie to get caught in the crossfires of this whole mess.

"Yes, sir, Sheriff."

"Smartass."

"Lame brain."

A smile curved his lips. "Love you, kiddo."

"Love you, too."

Ryder held the phone to his ear until the dial tone sounded. He always let his sister hang up first. A thing he did ever since he moved away from home. He never wanted to end a conversation in case she had more to say. Another aspect of becoming the man of the house before his time.

Worry still eating him, he placed another call, this one to Cupcakes Above the Clouds. Maggie texted a little while after he left the ranch to say she and Lizzy were headed into work at the bakery and were taking Kayla with them. It was a popular shop in the middle of town, so he hadn't been worried. Now that he knew David was searching for Kayla so openly, he was.

The phone rang once before it was picked up by Tony, the shop's part-time employee. "Cupcakes Above the Clouds. How may I help you?" he asked in his accented English.

"Hi, Tony. It's Sheriff Ryder."

"Sheriff Ryder, how are you? Would you like to place an order for the station?"

"No." As much as he would love to go by and see Kayla, he feared if he saw her, he wouldn't want to let her out of his sight again. "I was just hoping to talk with Kayla."

"*Señorita* Jenkins, *sí*. I will go and get her."

The young man was always so polite. The immigrant nephew of the Denning brothers' head ranch hand was trying to get citizenship. Tony was a hard worker who always lent a helping hand to those who needed it. Ryder wished the young man luck in his endeavors. He believed the kid would make a great asset to the country.

"Hello?"

Once he heard the sweet, melodic voice come on the line, the tension and fear filling his body evaporated. "Hey, sweetheart. How are you doing?"

"Great, actually. Lizzy and Maggie are really nice, and these cupcakes are amazing."

He chuckled, warmth filling him to hear her in such a cheerful mood. "I know. Maggie makes a mean cupcake."

"You're telling me. I've already eaten four, and I

would go for a fifth, but I don't want to spoil dinner. Maggie keeps talking about what she's going to make and it sounds delicious."

"If Maggie's making it, I'm sure it will be."

There was a pause. Then she asked in a soft voice, "Is everything okay?"

"Everything's fine." Not really, but he didn't need to worry her. He wanted to tell her about the APB and what his sister found out about David's past, but not over the phone. Later, when they were together, and alone. "I was just calling to check in. See how you were doing."

He heard a small sigh of relief. "I'm great."

"Good, good. I'll be by in a few hours to pick you up. Then we'll go to the Denning Ranch for dinner."

"I'll save you a cupcake. I helped Maggie make a batch of Mint Madness Cupcakes. She, um, said they were your favorite."

He could almost see the cute little blush that rose over her face when she got embarrassed.

"You made my favorite cupcake?"

"Well, I, ah, Maggie made them. I just helped."

He lowered his voice to a sexy growl. "Can't wait to taste them." *And you.* "I'll see you in a few."

He waited until she hung up, listening to the empty air space, imagining Kayla baking something special for him because it was his favorite. That *woman* was something special, and he was going to do everything in his power to keep her safe.

Chapter 17

"Elizabeth Hayworth, you put that cupcake down right now!" Maggie shrieked from across the kitchen.

Lizzy winked at Kayla. "You see, I told you she'd notice."

Kayla shared a grin with the saucy, pregnant woman as she placed the Caramel Surprise cupcake back into the cardboard take out box.

"You're no fun, Maggie."

"You've had six already," the baker complained with a frown.

"I'm eating for two."

"That baby needs more than sugary pastries to grow big and strong. I'm making my crockpot chicken potpie with a spinach salad for dinner tonight, and I don't want you to be full of sweets. My little niece or nephew cannot live on cupcakes alone. And neither can you."

"No, but it's sure delicious trying."

Kayla tried to smother her smile, but at Maggie's scowl, she followed Lizzy into howls of laughter.

Unable to fight them, the baker threw her hands up in the air. A smile cracked her frown, and soon she was joining in the gales of hilarity.

It was nice to laugh again. She hadn't laughed this hard since the movie she went to with Jen where the cops pretended to be college students.

At the reminder of her friend, and cops, her laughter died and tears gathered in the corner of her eyes. How could she be here laughing when Jen was gone?

It's not fair.

Her best friend should be here, too. If anyone in the world embodied the saying "full of life" it had been Jen. Happy, carefree, and so friendly…

"Hey, are you okay?"

At Maggie's question, she glanced up. The other two women had stopped laughing, their smiles turned down in concerned frowns. Oh great, now she was a party pooper. She hadn't meant to bring the mood down.

"I'm fine."

"Yeah, 'cause I always cry when I'm fine, too," Lizzy said with a snort. "Wait, scratch that. I actually cry all the time now for no reason at all, but I have my baby making hormones as an excuse. Fess up, honey. What's wrong?"

Maggie sent her friend a warning look, but Kayla didn't mind the mother-to-be's nosiness. In some ways, Lizzy reminded her of Jen.

Desperately needing that connection again, the bond of sisterhood, she answered as best she could. "I-I recently lost my best friend, and it's been tough without her."

Both women gasped.

"Oh you poor thing." Maggie grabbed her in a fierce hug.

She could do nothing to stop the tears from spilling over, and Lizzy reached over and handed her a tissue.

"Thank you." Pulling out from the embrace, she

dabbed at her eyes.

"You know, you two remind me of her, Jennifer. Jen was always so sweet, taking care of everyone, cooking meals." Her lips trembled with a shaky smile. "She was also the friendliest person I have ever met. If it wasn't for her, I would have spent every night sitting at home watching *Law and Order* reruns." Warmth entered her body as good memories washed over her. "Jen made me go out to bars, movies, art shows. She got me out of my element and into new things."

"Sounds like she was a wonderful person," Maggie said softly.

Lizzy nodded. "I wish we could have met her."

"She would have loved you both. Anyway, spending time with you guys today, it kind of felt like a little part of Jen was here with us."

The bell over the front door chimed. The shop had closed an hour ago. Which meant it could only be one person. Heartbeat racing, she wiped her eyes, trying to erase any evidence of her emotional outburst.

"Hello? Anybody here, or did Lizzy kick everyone out so she could eat all the cupcakes."

"I heard that Jake Ryder. No more cupcakes for you!"

He came around the corner, and Kayla's breath caught in her throat. His long, black hair was pulled back into a braid emphasizing the sharp jut of his cheekbones. It should have been feminine, but it wasn't. It made him look strong. The hard plains of his face fierce and beautiful, he looked good enough to eat. Strange, since she was in a place with the most scrumptious food she had ever tasted, and all she wanted to take a bite out of was the man standing ten feet away from her.

He leaned in to give Lizzy a little squeeze. "You know I'm only joking, honey. Hi, Maggie." He gave the other woman a brief hug as well.

"Hey, Ryder. How was work?"

At the mention of work, his smile dissipated. A dark cloud passed over his face, but it was gone in an instant. A small tremor of fear passed through her, but she pushed it away. He was the sheriff. If something bad happened at work, it didn't necessarily have to do with her situation.

"Nothing too exciting. Old man Miller's fence broke. He lost a few cows, but Tim and Jason found them. I called the guys at the lumber yard, and they agreed to donate some time and supplies next week to help Len fix his fence."

"Above and beyond, this guy."

"Yeah, Ryder, you're a regular hevior."

"That's not a word, Lizzy."

"Yes it is. Hero and savior all wrapped up in one fantastic package. Don't you agree, Kayla?"

Yes, she did.

The women were laying it on thick, but they didn't have to. She knew how amazing Ryder was. The man took her in without knowing who she was, opened his home to her, and when he discovered her secret, he promised to help her instead of turning her in. She still couldn't fully believe how amazing he was. Every morning, she expected to wake up in a cell, having dreamt this wonderful warrior and his willingness to help her.

"How are you doing, sweetheart?" he asked softly, coming to stand in front of her.

"I'm great."

His brow furrowed as he traced a finger down her still damp cheek. She reached up and grabbed his hand, squeezing reassuringly.

"Really, I'm okay."

Those chocolate brown eyes stared deeply into hers, like he was gazing into her soul. What was this connection between them? Deep and a little bit scary.

Without regard to their audience, he leaned down and placed a brief, but very hot, kiss on her lips. She didn't even get a chance to respond before he ended the connection and turned to the other women.

"You ladies need a ride back home?"

Both smiled with approval. Lizzy shook her head. "We drove in Maggie's car."

"Remember," the baker added. "You promised to come to dinner tonight. Kayla made dessert. Mint Madness cupcakes."

Ryder turned to her with a sexy grin on his face. "Yes, I know."

Heat rose up her cheeks, and her knees just about gave out.

"Then I guess we'll head out, unless you need any help closing up?"

Maggie waved him away. "No, we were actually done about fifteen minutes ago."

"Work goes a lot faster with an extra hand." Lizzy winked at her.

"See you at the ranch then." He took her hand in his own and headed toward the front.

"Not if we see you first," Lizzy called after them.

Kayla threw on her coat and followed him out into the cold. Ryder's truck was, thankfully, parked right out front. Her nose only froze a little before she once again settled in a warm, enclosed space.

"Are you sure you're okay?" he asked once they were on their way. "It looks like you've been crying."

She sighed, upset that she wasn't better at hiding her emotions. He was already doing so much for her. She didn't want to burden him with her roller coaster feelings, too. "Oh, it was nothing. I just forgot how wonderful it felt to have a best friend. Being with Maggie and Lizzy, well, it was almost like I was with Jen again. It feels like weeks have gone by since she died, not days."

"Death has a way of making time go wonky. It took me years before I stopped looking for Dad's car in the driveway at the end of the day."

Of course he would understand. How could she forget this man had lost people he loved, too? Placing a hand on his thigh, she patted softly. "I'm sorry, Ryder. I didn't mean to bring up bad memories."

He reached down, grasping her hand with his own and bringing it to his lips. A ripple of awareness shot through her as his mouth brushed against her skin.

"The only memories I have of my dad are good ones. Some are sadder than others, but they're all good."

They rode in silence for a moment, country music playing low on the radio, the crunch of snow under the tires. For the first time in days, a pleasant peacefulness settled over her.

"The girls invited me back to the shop tomorrow. Maggie says they're having a bit of a holiday rush and could use an extra hand."

"That's great." He released her hand and gripped

the wheel once more. "Actually, it's probably best if you don't spend too much time alone at my place."

The tone of his voice sent a spark of worry through her. He didn't want her to be alone, or he didn't want her alone in his house? Was he worried for her safety or had she over stepped her bounds with the kiss earlier?

Maggie and Lizzy assured her Ryder liked her, but what if they were wrong?

Oh, good grief. She felt like an adolescent relying on the word of her school chums on whether the cute boy in class had a crush on her. She'd always been terrible at reading signs as far as relationship stuff went. Had she misinterpreted Ryder?

He called her pet names like "sweetheart," but he also called Lizzy "honey" in the shop a little while ago. He was affectionate with her, kissing her hand or forehead. But again, she had seen him hug and be affectionate with the other women, too. Was she mistaking his friendliness for interest? Did he want her safe or away from him and his things?

But he'd kissed her in the shop. And not a *friendly* kiss. That kiss had felt like more, to her at least.

Maybe to me only?

Before she could ask him to clarify his meaning, they arrived at the Denning ranch. Ryder parked the truck in the large driveway and shut off the engine. Confused and worried, she unbuckled her seatbelt, trying her best to mask the emotions rioting inside. He came around the truck to open her door, offering her his hand to help her down. A romantic gesture or just more polite manners?

She was going crazy trying to figure this man out.

The night had already darkened, but the porch light

was on, illuminating their path to the front door. It opened to reveal…Colton, at least she believed that was the younger brother's name. The one with lighter hair, who was engaged to Maggie.

"Hey, guys. Come on in. Maggie and Lizzy should be here any—oh there they are."

Kayla turned, and sure enough, the headlights of Maggie's car shone bright behind them.

She quickly shuffled inside the house as the others followed. Hanging her coat on the rack, hellos were said. While kisses for the fiancés were exchanged, she turned her head, awkwardness heating her cheeks at witnessing such an intimate moment. Once the pleasantries finished, she followed Maggie and Lizzy into the kitchen

"I put everything in the crock pot this morning, so give me a few minutes and we can eat. You boys set the table."

"You got it, Magpie," Colton said, kissing his fiancée's neck.

Kayla shifted, unaccustomed with the intimate display. They sure were affectionate out here in Peak Town.

She helped with the salad while the men set the table and Lizzy took care of drinks—the only thing anyone would let the pregnant woman do in the kitchen.

The meal was delicious and the conversation lively. They talked about the upcoming holidays, the wedding, and Lizzy's next doctor appointment where they would discover the gender of the baby.

"Do you have a preference?" In her experience most people tended to.

"I don't care as long as it's healthy." Dade gazed at

his future wife with all the love in the world.

Kayla wondered what it would feel like to have someone stare at her like that.

Lizzy snorted. "What a load. Everyone has a preference, they just never say it in case they don't get what they want."

"Well, then what are you hoping for, Miss Sassypants?" Colton asked.

"A boy, of course. Everyone knows boys love their mommies. Besides, I remember when I turned thirteen and my hormones went crazy. Deal with that nightmare again? No thank you."

The pregnant woman had a point. As a teacher, she'd had to deal with a few puberty related meltdowns in the school hallways over the years. Thankfully, it didn't happen in her kindergarten class.

"Boys go through puberty, too, sweetheart."

"Yes, but if we have a boy, you get to deal with it, my love. Unless you want to explain to our daughter about the different types of sanitary devices?"

Kayla smiled at the look of pure terror on Dade's face. Colton thumped his brother on the back; their sibling ribbing made her wistful for that kind of playful familial connection.

"Relax, big bro, it won't be that bad. You can make a day of it and go shopping. Help little Lizzy Jr. pick out everything she needs."

"That sounds wonderful." Lizzy joined in on the teasing.

Dade narrowed his eyes at his brother. "I hope you have ten daughters, and they're all as flirtatious as you, you jackass."

Colton blanched, and the room burst out in

laughter. Kayla was enjoying herself immensely, but in the back of her mind she still worried. As much fun as it was having dinner and great conversation with her newfound friends, she had to remind herself this wasn't real. These people had no idea who she really was and why she was here. It would be so easy to pretend she was having a typical evening dinner with friends, like a normal person.

But she wasn't a normal person at the moment.

She also wanted to leave and get Ryder alone so they could finish their conversation. She needed clarification. If he didn't have romantic feelings for her then she needed to know.

So she could stop making a fool out of herself.

After dinner, they ate the Mint Madness cupcakes she helped make. Everyone commented on how delicious they were. Ryder kissed her temple, saying they were the best he had ever had. That had to be good, right?

Her emotions were in such turmoil by the time they were ready to leave, her stomach started to churn. The delicious dinner now sat like a cement rock in her gut.

A little after ten in the evening, they said their goodbyes, climbed back into Ryder's truck, and headed to his house.

The ride was quiet and tense. Not like the peaceful silence they rode in before. This was different.

Oh, no. She *had* misinterpreted his actions. He was just being his usual friendly self. What other explanation could there be for his sudden silence?

Kayla sneaked a glance at him from the corner of her eye. His face was tight, jaw clenched. Something was bothering him, it was clear. That something being her, she assumed.

She had been throwing herself at him when all he wanted to do was help her out. How could she be such an idiot? Why would Ryder want to be with her? She was a nobody, an average, plain Jane kindergarten teacher from Chicago turned framed wanted murderess of her best friend.

Every man's dream, right?

Ugh, such a moron.

This man, out of the kindness of his heart, wanted to help her out of her bad situation, and what does she do to repay him? Push herself on him like a pathetic, lovesick puppy. She should go ahead with her original plan and leave town. David was going to find her eventually. It would be better if she wasn't here when that happened; she'd already come to care too much for the people in this town to risk their lives.

The sudden stop of the car jarred her out of her thoughts. They had arrived back at his home, and she hadn't even realized it.

Before he could come around, she opened her door and slid out of the truck. She couldn't bare his politeness right now. Not when she was so humiliated by her behavior.

She led the way into the house. He locked the front door and threw his jacket on the back of the couch, still silent.

It was all too much for her.

"I'm sorry," she spoke, breaking the tense silence.

Tossing his boots on the shoe rack, Ryder glanced up at her in confusion. "For what?"

"For kissing you earlier." She rushed through her apology, hoping to get it all out without her entire body flushing from mortification. "I understand you're just being nice, trying to help me out. I didn't mean to…imply anything or embarrass you in front of your friends. I know you don't think of me that way and I—"

"What way?" he interrupted her ramblings.

"Um, the romantic way, I guess."

"Romantic way?"

"You know…in a, um, sexual way."

His eyes widened, and she wished the ground would open up and swallow her whole.

"You think I don't find you attractive?"

She shrugged. His dark gaze narrowed. He took a step toward her, then another, until she could feel his warm, chocolaty sweet breath on her face.

"You think I don't realize you're the most beautiful woman I have ever met, and with the strongest heart. You think I don't want to rip off every stitch of clothing on you and bury my body so deep inside we won't know where you end and I begin?"

She gasped, body throbbing at the vivid imagery he painted.

"Sweetheart, since the moment I met you, I've wanted nothing more than to strip you naked and sate myself in you until we're both blind from pleasure."

Her heart felt like it would burst from happiness. She'd been wrong. *So* wrong. He wasn't being polite— he did want her. Almost as desperately as she wanted him, it appeared.

"Yes." The soft word slipped out of its own accord.

He studied her, long and hard. "Are you sure, Kayla? Be sure, because once I have you, I'm not sure I'll be able to give you up."

Knowing there was no other answer, she wrapped

her arms around his neck, pulling him to her for a deep, hot, and very thorough kiss.

When she pulled away, she gazed right into those chocolate brown eyes, hazy with need, and said the only thing she could. "I am yours, Ryder. Have me."

Chapter 18

How in the world could Kayla think he didn't want her? How could he *not* want her? She was the strongest, bravest, most beautiful woman he had ever met. He would be an idiot if he didn't want her.

Ryder was trying to be noble. She had been through hell, she was vulnerable, the last thing she needed was him jumping on her like a dog in heat. He'd been trying to give her time. She needed to feel safe, not scared by his overwhelming desire for her.

Looking down at her needy, lust-filled eyes, he admitted she didn't appear scared, far from it, in fact. She struck him as a woman ready to go to bed, and not for the purpose of sleeping. She did ask him to have her...and he'd never been one to refuse a lady's request.

Bending down, he tucked an arm under her knees, scooping her up against his chest. Their gazes locked, never losing contact, as he walked down the hall to his bedroom. Kayla clung to him. Her delicate fingers teased his nape. Anticipation wound every muscle in his body tight. He would finally have her, tonight, right now.

The light was off in his bedroom, but the curtains were open. The full moon cast the room in a dim glow. Perfect. Just enough light so he could see every sweet curve of her body. Placing her gently on the bed, he kissed her again. She responded with fervor, sucking on his tongue, arching her tempting body against his. He was so hard right now he would bet he had an imprint of his zipper on his dick. He wanted to take her, hard and fast.

But he wouldn't.

This was Kayla. She was special. She deserved to be loved, thoroughly. He intended to give her a night of passion that would leave her spent and satisfied like no other woman before. Every inch of her would be worshiped by his hands, his mouth. He would discover what made her cry out in pleasure and moan in ecstasy.

Hard and fast could come later. They had all night.

Fisting the soft sweater in his hands, he tugged. She broke contact, lifting slightly to help him remove the garment. The short sleeve shirt underneath came off as well, leaving her bare from the waist up, except for the sexiest black bra he had ever seen.

"This is pretty." He traced the lace cups with a finger.

A soft moan escaped her lips. He watched as her nipples hardened, pressing against the lace, begging to be kissed. Bending his head, he did just that. She gasped as he closed his mouth over one stiff peak, tonguing the hard, round bud through the delicate material.

"Oh, Ryder, yes," she moaned, grabbing his head to press him against her.

Damn, this woman was hot. Every single thing she did turned him on.

Kayla gave a tiny yell as he bit gently on her nipple. One slim leg wound around him, pulling his lower half closer to hers. Releasing her breast, he blew across the damp cloth, causing her to shiver. He then turned his attention to the other breast, repeating the process and garnering another scream of ecstasy.

"Ryder?"

"Yes, sweetheart?" he asked, reluctantly leaving her perfect breast to look up at her.

"Will you take your hair out of the braid? Please?"

Women often commented on his long hair. Some liked it, some didn't. He never gave it much thought. It was how he wore it. The desire in her eyes shot straight to his soul, and he vowed right then and there to never cut his hair as long as this woman was in his life.

Reaching back, he pulled out the tie at the end of his braid and tossed it to the floor. Long, delicate fingers reached out, carefully weaving through his hair until it was free.

"It's so soft." Her gaze filled with wonder.

"You're soft. And sexy. And driving me insane." He punctuated each declaration with a kiss.

Kayla smiled. With fingers still running through his hair, she made another request. "Take off your shirt."

He thanked the powers that be he'd changed out of his uniform before picking her up that evening. Undoing all those buttons on his sheriff's shirt would have been more than he could handle at the moment.

Yanking a fistful of material, he had his chest bared in seconds. Her eyes widened, and her hands stopped playing in his hair to reach out to touch him. Every brush of skin felt like fire licking a path along his body where her fingers grazed.

"You're amazing."

"I'm just a man, sweetheart."

Her gaze rose to meet his.

"A man who needs you, desperately."

Her eyes went hazy, and she shifted against him. "I need you, too."

"Then let's get rid of the rest of these clothes so I can spend all night making sure your every need is met."

She gulped, beautiful hazel eyes going wide. "All night?"

He couldn't stop the grin curling his lips at her disbelieving expression. Reaching behind her back, he unhooked her bra, peeling the lace away. Her breasts were small, but perfect. He covered them with his hands.

Yes, perfect.

She sucked in a breath as he massaged and learned their intricacies. He could spend all night on her breasts, but he'd save that for another time.

Running his hand over her stomach, he flicked open the button of her jeans. The zipper rasped loudly in the still air as he gently pulled it down. "Lift up for me, honey."

She did, and he slid her jeans down her legs, tossing them to the floor.

"Now you."

Kayla reached for his belt, but he stilled her hands. "Not yet." He glanced down at the woman before him, clad only in black lacy panties. He could come right there just staring at her. God, she was a sight.

Beautiful, sexy, and so sweet.

"Ryder?"

Her hesitant question made him realize he had been staring.

"You are beautiful, Kayla."

She smiled, her entire face lighting up like he'd just given her the best gift in the world, and he felt ten feet tall. Knowing he put that beautiful expression on her face made him feel like a damn superhero.

He ran his hand up her bare legs, reveling in the silky feel of her smooth flesh. His thumbs stroked along the inside of her upper thigh, higher and higher until he came to the center of her. The sweetest spot known to man. He slipped one thumb inside her panties, rubbing soft circles right on that magic spot.

Her head fell back against the pillows as he stroked. "Oh, yes," she moaned loudly.

Damn, she was so sexy. He bent down, placing his mouth over her, tasting her through the cloth.

"Ryder, don't stop!"

Not a chance in hell.

Pushing the lace aside, he continued to rub while his tongue tasted her, delving inside to simulate what he would soon be doing to her with his cock. She tasted so sweet; he couldn't get enough.

All too soon, he felt her body tighten. She let out a cry of pleasure. He continued his ministrations even after she finished, working her up again, driving her to another peak. When she was almost to the crest, he pulled away.

"What?"

Without answering, Ryder quickly shucked his jeans and boxers. Reaching to his nightstand, he dug around, thanking his lucky stars when he found a condom. He ripped open the foil with his teeth.

Kayla's soft hand touched his, stopping him before he could put it on. "Let me."

He passed it to her and watched as she eyed him with hunger. Her hand reached out, grasping him softly, and he cursed at the sweet feel.

"You're big."

It wasn't a compliment, just a fact. He took it as such. "We'll fit."

"I know."

Then she wrapped her hand around him, stroking up and down once. It felt so good he nearly lost it. "Sweetheart, as amazing as that feels, you need to hurry up or I'm going to embarrass myself."

She giggled. "Nothing about you is embarrassing, Ryder. Trust me."

Slowly, a pleasurable torture, she rolled the condom on. About time. She burned him up so much he wasn't sure he could last much longer.

Taking her mouth in a deep, consuming kiss, he positioned himself at her entrance and slowly sank into her welcoming warmth. He slid in with ease, pressed deep inside until he couldn't go any farther.

Perfection. Being inside Kayla was as close to heaven as he had ever been.

He let out a harsh groan. "Damn, sweetheart, you feel amazing."

"So," she panted, "do you."

He moved then, slow, deep strokes. She matched his rhythm, and soon they were climbing together to that ultimate peak. Her fingers tangled in his hair, pulling him to her for another soul-consuming kiss. He quickened his thrusts. Her legs wrapped around him and he felt her inner muscles tighten.

Her mouth ripped away from his, and she screamed as her orgasm hit her full force. Ryder watched in awe;

2

it was a beautiful thing to see. But he could only enjoy it a moment before his own body tighten with release. He pumped into her twice more, hard, fast thrusts, before losing himself.

Ryder collapsed on bed, shifting them until he was lying on his back with Kayla splayed across his chest.

"Wow," she muttered, breath coming in harsh gasps.

"You can say that again."

"Wow!"

He chuckled, tucking her close, placing a kiss to her damp forehead. "Wanna take a shower?"

"I'd like that." She grinned up at him then rose, walking toward the master bath.

He watched the sway of her sexy ass.

"Oh, and Ryder?"

Reluctantly, he pried his gaze away from her backside to find her glancing at him over her shoulder, a wicked glint in her eyes.

"It's my turn to taste."

And just like that, he was ready to go again. He grinned, leaping from the bed to join her.

Oh yes, Kayla Jenkins was one amazing woman.

Chapter 19

David sat in the pathetic excuse for a motel room. The wallpaper was yellowed and peeling, the carpet smelled of smoke, and the spiders in the dingy bathroom outnumbered him a dozen to one. Disgusting, and not his standard travel preference. He preferred hotel suites with fully stocked mini bars and in-room Jacuzzi tubs. He was used to the best. Growing up, his family always had money, and they flaunted it with pride.

This room wasn't a step down from his norm, it was a free fall plunge into the abyss. But it was cheap, right off the highway, and accepted cash with the name Mr. Smith. Right now, he needed the anonymity. So, this shitty room would have to do.

After reviewing the footage at the drug store in Kansas, he'd come up with a plan and sent out an APB to every police station within fifteen hundred miles, every station *except* for those in Illinois. If Chief Vic discovered he was trying to find Kayla himself, without sharing any information with the station, the old man would have his ass.

And possibly his badge.

But he needed to find Kayla, *before* anyone else. He couldn't allow her to talk, tell her side of the story. Highly unlikely anyone would believe her, but all it took was one shred of doubt and the investigation could turn toward him. David couldn't allow that to happen.

So, he'd sent out the APBs from his private computer. It wasn't hard to mock up a document to look official. The Internet was a very helpful tool. A man could find instructions for anything on there. He was no computer geek, but he could use a search engine and Photoshop.

A shrill chime from his phone alerted him to an incoming call.

"Tyler," he answered, putting the phone to his ear.

"Hey, it's Perry."

Speaking of computer geeks. Perry Lang was a mid-level hacker who did favors for him in exchange for letting the guy off the hook when he got busted for identity theft. He'd covered Lang's ass, and now the time had come for Lang to return the favor.

"What do you have for me?" No small talk among men like them.

"I ran the photo you sent me through my feeds."

Lang had access to some satellite thing with facial recognition around the country. Most likely illegal, but David didn't care. If it found Kayla, that was all that mattered.

"Did you find anything?"

"Not yet."

He gripped the phone tighter, temper rising. "Then why the hell are you calling?"

A whimper came from the other end. The guy had the guts of a goldfish, but David didn't need his guts. He needed the geek's computer skills.

"Well, um, I didn't find her yet, but I did find something else."

"What?" The single word ripped from his throat.

His patience was on a short fuse.

"Someone's been looking into your files."

Sonofabitch! "Who?"

The sound of fingers clacking against a keyboard came over the line before Lang responded. "Some lawyer in Colorado. Julie Ryder. Looks like she got access to your juvenile record."

What the hell? That record was supposed to be sealed. His father's lawyer assured him it would never see the light of day. Bloodsucker got paid enough to shoot that thing into space—*how the hell did some country-ass lawyer get her hands on it?*

"Why the hell is she digging into my past?" That was the more important question right now.

"I don't know." The fear in his voice came through the phone loud and clear. "I just know she got the information."

There was only one explanation, Kayla had managed to convince the lawyer she was innocent, and now this Julie Ryder was looking into his history to prove he was capable of killing Jen. The sealed record couldn't be used in a court of law; still, if the bitch found it, then it stood to reason she could find out other things. The bribes, the other women he paid not to talk, there were any number of dark deeds someone could find if they were looking hard enough.

Fuck!

"Get me everything on this lawyer." His hand gripped his phone in a bruising hold, rage burning through every inch of his body. "I want to know where she lives, who her family is, what she eats for goddamn breakfast! You hear me?"

"Ye—yes," Lang stammered. "I'm on it—"

David hung up while the nervous geek was still stuttering out his response. Screaming with fury, he ripped the lamp from the nightstand and sent it hurtling across the room. It hit the wall, shattering into dozens of pieces.

Shit, shit, shit!

Things were getting out of hand. He needed to find Kayla and silence the bitch, *now*. It looked like he was going to have to take care of the lawyer, too. Shouldn't be too hard. Colorado, huh? They had snowy mountain roads out there, right? An icy road, dark night, high mountain pass with no guardrails, the perfect accident. If he got really lucky, the bodies would never be found.

Grabbing his bag, he said goodbye to the shitty motel room and arachnid roommates, got in his car, and pulled onto the highway. He could take I-70 all the way to Colorado. Once Lang found Julie Ryder's address, he'd set his plan in motion.

He turned on the radio to John Denver's melodic voice belting out "Rocky Mountain High." David smiled. It was a sign. In his mind, he imagined Kayla's eyes widening with fear as she tumbled off a fifty-foot cliff.

Rocky mountain high, indeed.

Chapter 20

Kayla woke in the middle of the night. At least, she thought it was the middle of the night as darkness shrouded the room. Ryder had closed the curtains before they fell asleep, but no sunlight peeked in around the cloth, so she figured it was still nighttime.

His strong arms were wrapped around her. They felt warm and safe and something else…something she wasn't used to. There was some emotion deep inside her she couldn't name. Or didn't want to name. If she was feeling what she suspected, it would create more problems than she had already. And she had *a lot* of problems right now.

Best not to dwell on it too much. Better to live in the moment and enjoy.

Boy oh boy, is there a lot to enjoy.

Ryder was a very thorough lover. She didn't have much experience when it came to relationships—a few long-term boyfriends and one disastrous one-night-stand she'd indulged in after a particularly nasty break up. It had been Jen who convinced her to "snag a rebound lay." One of her friend's few bad ideas.

A warm, wet, tear rolled down her cheek. Would she ever be able to remember her friend without crying? She hoped so. There so many good memories. One day, she wanted to think of Jen and smile.

For now, perhaps a cold drink would help. She *was*

a bit thirsty, all that energy expended earlier. Warmth of another kind rose inside her as she remembered everything she had done and had been done to her. Ryder spent hours making love to her. Never in her life had she felt so sexy, desired, and cherished. He found trigger spots on her body she didn't even know existed. The man was a veritable sex god.

Carefully, so as not to wake him, she slipped from his arms and tiptoed across the room.

"Where you sneaking off to?" The sleepy rumble came from the bed she just vacated.

"I'm sorry. I didn't mean to wake you. I was going to get a glass of water. Would you like one?"

He rose on one elbow. The blanket fell to his waist, exposing his bare chest. A chest she'd memorized with her tongue earlier. She swore she could still feel all those hard planes and muscles, taste all that delicious, utterly male flesh. Her body temperature elevated at the memory.

Okay, now I really need a cold drink.

"Sure, I could use a rejuvenator." A heated gleam entered his gaze.

"You're insatiable."

He grinned, giving her a wink. "Sweetheart, you're just too tempting. Now, go get that water before I decide I can't wait and take you again."

As lovely as that sounded, she really was thirsty. Plus, she needed a minute to gather her thoughts. This thing with Ryder was all happening so fast. They only met a few days ago—not to mention under extreme circumstances.

He was helping her out with the whole David situation, letting her live with him, and now they were intimate. A small part of her warned she was relying on him too much. As someone who always had to rely on nobody but herself, it was a very new and strange experience. She'd never had anyone take care of her the way Ryder did. It felt wonderful and a little scary. She didn't want to start depending on him only to lose him.

What happened if David found her or someone turned her in? And if she *could* somehow prove David was guilty, what then? She'd go back to her life in Chicago, and Ryder...he had his life here. Long distance rarely worked.

She made her way down the hallway to the kitchen, thoughts of relationships, murders, and happily-ever-afters consuming her. Though what she wore was one of Ryder's black T-shirts, which fell to her knees, the thin material did nothing to keep out the cold night air. As she passed by the living room, she noticed Ryder's discarded jacket thrown over the back of the couch. She grabbed it, stuffing her arms into the sleeves.

Much better.

Kayla pulled the coat around her and inhaled deeply, letting his scent envelope her. Woodsy with a hint of coffee. *Mmmmmm.*

She started toward the kitchen when something slipped from the pocket of the coat. Intending to simply return the paper from where it fell, she bent down and grabbed the corner. It unfolded in her fingers...and she froze.

Terror gripped her. Unable to move, she stared at her last year's staff photo below the words: *Wanted for Suspected Murder.* There in black, glaring typeface was all her information: height, weight, hair, eye color, and...

...extremely dangerous and may be armed.
Oh no!

Ryder said they didn't get news like this out here in Peak Town, but this proved him wrong.

...please contact Officer David Tyler of the Chicago Police Department.

David was looking for her. *David* specifically, because the number at the bottom was his cell phone—the same one Jen had taped up on the fridge in case Kayla ever needed it.

"You digging a well for that water or what?"

She jumped at Ryder's smooth voice and tore her gaze away from the paper she held to look up at him.

"Kayla? What's wrong, baby? You're white as a ghost."

Gripping the APB tight in her hand, she held it up. "He's looking for me."

He glanced at the paper then ran a hand through his long, unbound hair. "Shit."

"Not the Chicago PD. *David.* See this number at the bottom? It's not the station's. It's David's. I recognize it." She was rambling, she knew, but what else were you supposed to do when the man who had killed your best friend and framed you appeared to be out on a vendetta killing? She'd like to see anyone else keep their cool in this situation.

"I know."

"You know...?"

Of course he knew. Ryder was the sheriff, had been at work all day. The paper fell from his jacket. He knew David was looking for her, and yet, he'd said nothing, all night. What did that mean?

A cold sense of dread filled her. She closed her

eyes, trying to block out the terror of the situation. Her heartbeat raced, breath shuttering in harsh pants. Had he changed his mind? Did he think she was guilty after all? Did he intend to turn her in? Was this whole night just a way to keep her distracted until David showed up to haul her away...or worse, kill her?

The paper started to shake in her tight grip.

"Stop it." The words were a growl in the darkness. "Right now."

She opened her eyes to find him mere inches in front of her. How had he moved without her hearing?

His brown eyes narrowed; his sculpted jaw clenched tight. Those amazing lips, which only hours ago had teased and tormented her body into mind-numbing bliss, now flattened with disappointment.

"Stop what?" Her heart pounded in her chest. The fear all-consuming. What was she going to do?

"Stop thinking I turned you in. I can see it on your face, Kayla." He shook his head when her jaw dropped in shock. "How could you think, after what happened between us tonight, I would ever hurt you like that?"

She didn't know what to say, didn't know what to believe.

"I don't care what this paper says, I believe *you*. I know you didn't kill your best friend." When she still remained mute, he took her face in his hands. Leaning down, he placed a hard and fast kiss to her lips. "I care about you, dammit."

He kissed her again, soft this time. Pressing his lips against hers. Savoring her as if she was special, as if she mattered.

"More than I've cared about anyone, ever." His voice was softer when he spoke again.

She sucked in a breath as her pounding heart leapt into her throat. Still, she stayed silent, words eluding her.

"I didn't tell you about the APB because I didn't want you to worry. I'm sorry."

She placed her free hand on his wrist, staring deeply into those chocolate brown eyes, finally finding her voice. "I care about you, too."

He smiled, dipping his head again for another kiss, this one less sweet and more carnal. When he lifted his head, she licked her lips, still tasting him on her tongue.

"Come on, I think we need something a bit stronger than water now."

He led her into the kitchen and sat her at the table. Kayla dropped the paper—with her face and "wanted for murder" written all over it—on the table.

He handed her a glass of dark liquid. She sniffed, the smell burning her nostrils, and took a small sip.

Oh, gaw! What the heck is this stuff, motor oil? Her throat burned like fire. Whatever he gave her tasted awful.

"Sorry," he said with a sheepish grin. "All I have is whiskey."

Whiskey? Blech! She was more a vodka girl. Martini with olives was how she rolled. This stuff tasted like paint stripper.

"How about a little cola to go in that?"

She nodded, pushing her glass toward him. Ryder grabbed it and went to the fridge to retrieve the soda.

"What does this APB mean for me?" she asked. "What's the plan?"

He set her drink on the counter, popping the top off the can, and filling the rest of the glass with the fizzy beverage.

"Nothing, it means nothing. No one else saw this, so no one knows. You're still safe here, Kayla."

He came back to the table and handed her the doctored drink. She took a small sip.

"Better?"

A little. She'd never order this at a bar, but Ryder was trying to help her calm down, so she simply smiled and nodded.

"Liar." He grinned back, shaking his head. "You don't have to drink it if you don't want to, sweetheart."

"It's fine, really. Thank you."

He watched her for a moment then shrugged. "I agree that it appears David is looking for you on his own, which means he doesn't want his superiors to know he's on your trail."

"How do we know he's on my trail?"

"We don't, but if this got to Peak Town, there's a good chance he's reaching out to a specific area. Is there any trail for him to follow? Did you buy plane tickets or stay in a motel under your name?"

She took another drink. The distasteful liquor concoction started to taste better. Shaking her head, she replied, "No. I didn't stay in any motels, and I took a bus, paid cash."

He rubbed his chin in thought.

"Although…"

"What?"

She grimaced, remembering her fear in the terminal. "There was a security camera. In the bus station in Kansas. It might have gotten a shot of me."

Ryder downed half of his whiskey in one sip.

Good grief, the man must have a stomach of steel.

"Okay, so assuming he saw the footage, we can presume he sent this out to every police station in a one to two thousand mile radius. Except the stations in Illinois, of course."

"Why not there?"

"He wouldn't want his boss to know what he was doing." He paused a moment in thought. "Unless his boss is dirty, too."

She shook her head. "I've met Chief Vic. He's a hard man, but fair. I don't think he's dirty." Then again, she didn't think David was capable of murder, so what did that say about her judgment of people?

Ryder ran his finger around the lip of his glass. "Hmmm, still, I better have Liam look into him, too."

"Who's Liam?" Her palms started to sweat.

"Old police academy buddy. He's FBI now."

She shot out of her seat. "You told the FBI where I was?"

"Calm down, sweetheart." Ryder lifted his hands as if she was a wild animal.

Right now, she sort of felt like one—a trapped one.

"I didn't tell him about you. I have him looking into David's background. We need evidence of Tyler's temper if we're going to prove he killed Jen."

Her heart raced. All this stress was going to give her a heart attack, she was sure of it. Grabbing her drink, she downed it in one swallow. Fire burned a path down her throat into her stomach. She focused on the burn, letting it take over and push everything else out.

"So far, he hasn't found anything, but he's still looking. Julie found something—"

"Julie? As in *your sister*?" She choked around her heated throat. "You have your sister looking into David, too?"

More people involved meant more lives on the line. More people for David to target.

She paced the kitchen, fearing she had doomed all these kind people to a crazy murder's wrath. "No, no, no. Ryder you can't. I never should have come here. I never should have let you talk me into staying."

Anger darkened his face as he stood. "So, you should have what? Kept running?"

"*Yes*," she screamed, frustrated that this man didn't understand her dilemma.

"Great plan, Kayla. When I found you, you were half-frozen, lost in the woods. Are you saying I should have left you there to die?"

"Yes. You should have left me. Instead, you brought me here and got your friend involved...and your sister. When David finds me, he's going to kill me and anyone who tried to help me." Tears spilled down her face; she could do nothing to stop them. "I don't want anyone to die because of me."

Ryder reached out, pulling her into his arms. She let herself go, reveling in the warm safety he offered. She shouldn't be doing this. She needed to leave. To protect the man she was rapidly falling in love with and his loved ones, she had to leave and take her troubles with her. It wasn't fair to put them on Ryder.

"So," he spoke softly against her hair, "you're saying your life isn't as important as mine? Because, honey, I have to disagree with you there."

"You have people who love you, people who depend on you." She sniffed against his chest. "I'm an orphan whose best friend was killed less than a week ago. No one would miss me if I'm gone," her voice cracked with the softly spoken confession.

"*I* would." His voice broke as he held her tight. "You're not alone anymore, Kayla. You have me."

Then his lips were on hers, tasting, taking, loving. His hands slipped under the oversized T-shirt, running up and down her body, setting it alight with fire. He backed her up until her backside hit the table, then he grabbed her and lifted, placing her back down on top of the polished oak.

"*I* care about you, Kayla, and I will never let anyone hurt you. Ever again."

His words were a vow. One she didn't want to look into so deeply right now. At the moment, she wanted Ryder, inside her, filling her with his strength.

"I need you, Ryder. Now."

She reached for him, dipping her hand into the soft cotton pajama bottoms to find him waiting for her, hard and ready. Gripping his cock, she pumped up and down. He felt amazing, so soft and yet so hard at the same time. His dark eyes flared with heat as he gazed down at her. His fingertips played between her legs, testing her, preparing her.

One hand reached into the pocket of his pajamas and produced a foil wrapper.

Oh, so that's why men's pajamas have pockets. How handy.

In less than a second, he had the package open. She took the condom from him and rolled it on his length. When she released him, he crushed his lips to hers, thrusting his tongue into her mouth. She clutched his shoulders as he opened her with his fingers and drove home in one deep plunge.

No soft and sweet this time. This was a battle. As if

Ryder was trying to prove something with this lovemaking. His mouth devoured her, and his body took her to the highest peak of pleasure. The assault on her senses was overwhelming. Every thrust sent him in deeper, every retreat made her want more. In only a matter of minutes, she felt her body tighten and explode in the most amazing release she had ever had, causing her to wrench her lips from his and scream his name. He pumped into her twice more before shouting out his own finish.

They sat there in the aftermath, breathing heavily, partially disrobed and sweaty, foreheads pressed together, her shirt tangled around her shoulders. Ryder's pants had fallen to his ankles.

"I don't think this was the intended purpose for this table." She gave a small laugh.

He pulled back, eying her devilishly. "You're right."

Gently, he laid her down on the surface. Then he pulled her hips to the edge and went to his knees. Bobbing his brows, he gave her a wicked smile. "It was meant for feasting."

Chapter 21

Sweeping up cupcake crumbs from the shop floor, Kayla smiled, noting how quickly the week had passed. They didn't speak about David or the APB again. Ryder told her he still had his friend and sister looking into the crooked cop. He assured her one of them would eventually uncover something that would help lead them to David's guilt.

She wasn't going to hold her breath. David was one slick bastard.

In the meantime, she spent her days at the Denning Ranch or at the cupcake shop. She was becoming fast friends with the two women. Lizzy and her outrageous personality and Maggie with her sweet, nurturing attitude, not to mention all the yummy cupcakes she could eat, who wouldn't be taken in? Kayla even liked Colton and Dade. The brothers were true cowboys, strong, kind, gallant. Not too bad in the looks department either. And they adored their fiancées, showering the women with love every chance they got. That alone got them gold stars in her book.

Her nights were filled with Ryder. He would pick her up after work, they'd head to his house and make dinner, then spend hours making love. Some nights they stopped to watch a movie or play cards. One night, he even tried to get her to ride Wind Chaser again, but she distracted him from the idea by removing her clothing.

She had nothing against the horse, but the animal was huge. She'd stick to a merry-go-round thank you very much.

In between worshiping each other's bodies, they talked. He shared more about the pain of losing his father, the pressure he felt becoming the man of the house, the need to look after his mother and sister. When his mother passed, he was both happy and sad, happy she was reunited with his father, but also grieving the loss of his only remaining parent.

It felt as if she'd known him for years.

Kayla shared her past, too. The sadness she grew up with knowing no one wanted her. The good homes she hated to leave, the bad ones she couldn't wait to escape. Ryder held her as she talked, whispering comforting words in her ear, telling her how strong she was. He made her feel safe, cherished, wanted, and made her want him and this life in return...

But she couldn't have it. As long as David and the Chicago Police were looking for her, she could never have a normal life.

"Hey, Tony," she said, pulling herself away from her thoughts. "What do you have there?"

The young man blushed. When he smiled, she noticed twin dimples. *This one is going to be a heartbreaker.*

"Oh, it is a care package for my friend, Jamie."

"You mean *girl*friend." Lizzy made a catcall sound from her desk in the back of the shop. They had locked up and were doing nightly closing duties.

Tony blushed deeper, his dark skin flushing with a red hue. "We are just friends, Ms. Lizzy."

"Jamie used to work here part time," Maggie

explained from her position at the sink. "She went off to college this past fall. Harvard."

Kayla bent down and swept the pile of cupcake crumbles into the dustpan then tossed them into the garbage. "Harvard? Wow, that's impressive. Really far away though."

"Yes, she is very intelligent and beautiful. I cannot imagine her having trouble making friends. But she told me she was missing home, so I thought sending her some of her favorite cupcakes might cheer her up."

She wondered if the young man realized he called Jamie beautiful. He could protest all he wanted, but she suspected there was much more than friendship there.

"That's so thoughtful of you, Tony." Maggie wiped her hands on her apron. "Next time you talk to Jamie, tell her I say hi, okay?"

"I will, Ms. Maggie. Do you need anything else from me tonight?"

"No. I think we're all done for today. Go on home. Hey, when is your citizenship test? I thought you said it was coming up soon, right?"

Tony nodded. "After the holidays."

"Well, let me know if you need any help studying. I mean it, Tony. Don't be afraid to ask for help."

"Yeah," Lizzy chimed in. "We're all rooting for you. Any help you need, let us know."

"Thank you. Goodnight, Ms. Lizzy, Ms. Maggie, Ms. Kayla."

Tony clutched the small box tightly to his chest and headed out the back door. Kayla stared after him with an amused grin.

"That boy is so polite." Maggie said.

Lizzy snorted. "Yeah, at least I got him to drop the

last names, finally."

"He's sweet. Are he and your former employee truly *just* friends?"

The small baker untied her apron and hung it on the wall hook. "I think so, although, it's clear both of them want more."

"Yeah," Rubbing a hand over her round belly, Lizzy shook her head. "But long distance relationships rarely work. Especially when you're as young as those two. Jamie is off at college studying and experiencing new things. Tony is going for his citizenship. Their lives are kind of going in different directions."

Her heart sank. Not only for Tony, such a nice boy in the deep stages of a first love, but also for herself. Tony and Jamie's situation brought her and Ryder's into stark parallel. Sure, she was here now, but with this thing with David and her murder charge...? And if they did manage to beat David...what would happen to her and Ryder when she went back to her life in Chicago?

She'd be lying if she said the idea of staying hadn't crossed her mind. It had. Like ten times a day. There had been nothing special about Chicago, she'd simply got a full ride to the University of Illinois, so that's where she went. A teaching job in the city came right after school. She loved her job, but she could teach anywhere. Good teachers were in high demand in every part of the country.

And now that Jen's gone—

Her eyes misted. The pain from the loss of her friend stung like a sore that wouldn't go away. She kept reliving it, unable to stop prodding at the open wound because of her situation. She wished this whole thing with David was resolved and over so she could finally deal with Jen's death and start healing. Maybe then the ache would lessen. Deep in her heart, though, she knew it would never fully go away.

No, she had no ties to Chicago anymore. She could leave if she wanted. Move anywhere, even a small, charming, little mountain town in Colorado. Still, there was the fact Ryder had not asked her to move here. They had never discussed it, truthfully. They talked about their pasts a lot, but never their future. Did that mean this was just a fling? He cared about her, she knew. He said it time and time again. But caring for her didn't mean he wanted something permanent.

"You never know, Lizzy. Long distance can work sometimes."

Maggie's voice snapped Kayla out of her morose ponderings. All this talk of love and long distance was wearing on her already heavy heart.

"So, Lizzy, tomorrow's the day you find out the gender right?" she asked, trying to change the subject.

The pregnant woman perked up. "Yes, I am so excitvous I could burst."

She glanced to Maggie, sharing a grin before saying together. "That's not a word."

"Excited and nervous." Lizzy stuck out her tongue. "We're having the doctor put the gender in a sealed envelope. I'm going to give it to Maggie, and she's going to make blue or pink cupcakes, depending on the results."

"Ooooo, sounds like fun."

"You and Ryder should come over for dinner tomorrow night for the big reveal."

"I'd love to. Let me check with him and get back to you."

"Check with me about what?"

She turned at the sexy, familiar voice behind her. "Ryder." The man really was quiet as a mouse. "When did you get here?"

"Just now."

He walked over and bent to kiss her. Soft and sweet and over too soon. Still, Lizzy and Maggie were grinning like idiots when Ryder released her.

"Oh, shut up, you two."

Her new friends burst into laughter, so infectious she had to join in. It felt good to have a friend again. Not only one, but two. How lucky could a woman get?

"You ready to go?" Ryder whispered in her ear.

Hot chills raced up and down her spine. *Luckier. Much, much luckier.*

"Maggie and Lizzy invited us to dinner tomorrow night. They're going to reveal the gender of the baby."

"Sounds exciting. Count us in."

He wrapped his arms around her waist, and she settled against his chest, enjoying the feel of his hard, strong body surrounding her.

"Can we bring anything?"

"Just yourselves," Maggie said.

"Will do. See you ladies tomorrow. Come on, sweetheart. Let's go home."

She reluctantly left his embrace to place the broom and dustpan back where they belonged, trying hard not to think about how good it felt to hear him say those three little words.

Let's go home.

****

David closed the door on another shitty motel room. This one just off of the shady end of downtown

Denver, Colorado. He'd been staying here three days waiting for Lang to get back to him—three days too long. He'd just begun to think the hacker was losing his edge when, finally, that morning, he received a text message with an address for one Ms. Julie Ryder.

The time has come.

He jumped into his car, ignoring the pock-marked guy trying to sell him "mind candy" and the forty year old trying to pass for twenty offering him a "date." This part of town was goddamn disgusting. But it was a place no one would look for him, so that was where he hid out.

No more hiding, he thought with a grin. Time to put his plan into action.

He still didn't know where Kayla was, but he'd bet his well-padded inheritance Julie Ryder did. All he needed to do was find the lawyer bitch and have a nice *friendly chat* with her.

He peeled out of the parking lot and headed toward the highway.

Next stop, Aspen, Colorado. Julie would tell him where Kayla was, or he'd make her suffer.

He chuckled to himself. Who was he kidding? That bitch would suffer anyway. They both would. Then, they would die.

Nobody messed with David Tyler. *Nobody.*

Chapter 22

"Kayla, honey. Wake up."

Soft lips brushed against her ear. She moaned, in that sweet state of not quite awake but not fully asleep, and rolled to her side, reaching for Ryder. Kayla slid her hands down his firm chest and around to his fantastic buns of steel. The man's backside was seriously yummy. She'd bet you could even bounce a quarter off it.

He chuckled in her ear. The vibrations moved through her body, causing tingles of awareness to spark between her legs.

"As much as I would love to stay and finish this little exploration of yours, sweetheart, I'm afraid I have to go."

She opened her sleepy eyes, trying to focus in the dim morning light. "Go?"

Long, dark hair shifted as he nodded. "I just got a call. Drunk driver swiped a minivan."

That woke her up faster than a bucket of cold water. "Oh, no! Is everyone okay?"

He nodded. "Yeah, sounds like. The EMT's are there, along with my deputy, Tim. But he cut himself pretty bad pulling the guy out of the wrecked car. The paramedics are taking him to county for stitches, so I need to go take the driver in for processing and lock up."

She nodded. "I understand. Be safe out there, okay?"

Delicious full lips smiled. "I was more concerned with you." A grimace replaced the smile. "I don't like leaving you alone with David out there. Do you want me to call the Denning ranch, see if Colton or Dade can swing by?"

She looked at the bedside clock and shook her head. "It's three in the morning. I don't want to disturb them." A slight tremble of fear rumbled low in her belly at the thought of being alone, but it had been over a week with no sign of David closing in on her. She didn't want Ryder thinking she couldn't take care of herself. At his concerned gaze, she pressed. "I'll be fine, Ryder, really."

"You sure?"

Reaching up, she sank her hands into his long, silky, dark hair, pulling him to her for a scorching kiss.

"Damn, sweetheart. You sure make it hard to leave."

She giggled at the husky tone in his voice. "I promise I'll be fine. Go on now, Sheriff. Your town needs you."

His gaze locked onto hers, his expression more serious than she had ever seen on him before.

"And what about you? Do you need me?"

Her smile froze, and the way he said that…it didn't sound like a throwaway question. Not a temporary need, but a permanent one. It sounded to her as if Ryder was asking if she needed him in her life, long-term. Her heart thumped a tango in her chest.

Crazy. Just her wayward imagination running away with her. The sad, little dreams of an unwanted child searching for a place to call home. He didn't mean it the way she hoped. How could he? They had barely known each other two weeks. He was just being his sweet, concerned self, making sure she was okay with staying in his home alone. Nothing more. She would do well to remember that fact.

"I'll be fine. Go." Unable to face him while she avoided his question, she turned over on her side then and snuggled back into the warm covers.

Their warmth was diminished when Ryder left the bed. She could hear the shuffling of clothing, the clink of a belt. Then he sat behind her again, most likely fully clothed in his uniform. The bed dipped with his weight as he leaned over and kissed her temple.

"I'll call later to check in. Kayla, I—"

He paused, and she held her breath; the moment felt heavy, expectant.

"Call me on my cell if you need anything."

Then he was gone.

Kayla listened to the open and close of the front door and tried not to let her disappointment swallow her. What had she expected? A declaration of love? Stupid, why would he say he loved her? She was letting her emotions fly away again. Ryder was a great guy, a helpful, kind man. They had chemistry, there was no doubt, but that didn't translate to love.

Just because she might be falling—*okay, let's be honest, there is no* might be *about it.* She had been falling in love with Ryder ever since the first moment she looked up in those cold, snowy woods and had seen a warrior on horseback come to save her.

Years of rejection caused her to be a coward when it came to love. Jen always said she never dated a man she could ever get serious about, and that's why the relationships always ended. Her best friend had been right. Kayla was terrified when it came to love. Her mother abandoned her, she never even knew her father, and no one had ever wanted to adopt her. Some of the foster homes included her in family celebrations, but none of them wanted her to be a *permanent* part of their family.

No one had ever wanted her. A fact drilled into her since her birth. How could she take a chance on love when it had never taken a chance on her?

Tears slipped from her eyes, sliding down her cheeks to form small wet spots on the pillow. Her heart broke, because she knew to the depths of her soul she did love Ryder. She loved him more than she ever imagined it possible to love another person. It terrified her—though she may love him, she had no idea if he loved her. And that deep-seated fear of rejection kept her from asking. If she told Ryder of her feelings and he didn't reciprocate, it would be another in a long line of people who didn't want her.

And honestly, she didn't think her heart would survive a rejection from the only man she ever loved.

Chapter 23

David waited in the shadows of Julie Ryder's apartment building. His informant sent him a picture of her, so when a bright red SUV parked in the lot and a tall, dark-haired woman stepped out, he knew it was the lawyer. Seething anger burned in his gut.

This is the woman digging shit up? He snorted— one strong gust of wind would knock her over...or one strong punch in the face.

His knuckles cracked as he tightened his fist. Pulling back on his rage, he waited until she started down the sidewalk before he stepped out of the shadows. Her head was down, attention on her phone, so it was easy to casually bump into her shoulder.

"Oh, excuse me," he said, turning on the charm and giving her the smile he used to set people's nerves at ease.

Big brown eyes widened as she glance up to his face. "No, my fault entirely. Really. I should pay more attention to where I'm going."

Yes, she should, but it played out well for him that she was as obtuse as everyone these days, attention always where it wasn't supposed to be.

"You sure you're all right then?"

She stared at him, gaze narrowing. A prickle of unease tingled at the back of his neck.

Shit, what if she recognizes me?

He hadn't thought of that. The lawyer had been looking into his past; it stood to reason she knew what he looked like. He'd planned on running into her and casually finding out what she knew, but with that searching look in her eyes, he knew he had to move to plan B.

"Miss?"

She shook her head, and he breathed a sigh of relief when she didn't reveal her knowledge of him.

"Yes, I'm fine. Thank you."

"Have a pleasant day."

"You, too," she called after him as he continued down the sidewalk.

He headed in the opposite direction, stopping once he heard her enter the building. Using the stealth he'd honed on stakeouts, David turned and made his way back to the front door. He glanced in the small window by the side of the door. A tiny lobby with rows of mailboxes lay just beyond the door. Julie stood there talking to some old hag with the butt ugliest dog he had ever seen in the old lady's arms.

He watched as the women chatted back and forth. Julie reached out to pet the fat, flat-faced dog. It sneezed and licked her hand. Patience wearing thin, he had to restrain himself from barging in there. What the hell could they be talking about for so long? He needed to get Julie alone, quickly, before someone else came by. He knew he looked suspicious standing out here peering into the window.

If they didn't break up this chat fest soon, he'd have to go into the building anyway. He couldn't have someone call the cops to report a peeping Tom. Just as he contemplated making his move, the older woman grabbed her mail and turned, waving with the freaking dog's paw.

A sigh of relief left him. As Julie made her way down the hall, he quietly snuck in the front door, following her. Her apartment was all the way at the end of the building. He couldn't believe his luck, the positioning made what he planned all the easier. As she unlocked the door and turned the knob, he slid up behind her

"Julie Ryder?"

She glanced over her shoulder, confusion then recognition entering her gaze.

"Oh, you again. How did you know my name?"

He smiled, but this wasn't a pleasant smile like the one before. This time he let his true nature show in the curve of his lips. Her dark gaze widened as it finally hit her who he really was.

"David Tyler." Her voice trembled as she spoke his name. "What are you—"

He slapped the wet cloth he'd kept in his jacket pocket for just this emergency over her face, ending whatever the hell she planned on saying. She struggled, kicking and hitting at anything she could. He'd dealt with people resisting arrest before, so it was easy to avoid her attacks. Nothing made purchase. He shoved her through her open door, holding the cloth firmly over her mouth and nose. Slamming the door closed with his foot, he dragged her into the apartment as her body went limp.

She wouldn't be out for long, and he needed to get her out of there. He couldn't do what he needed to do to make her talk in an apartment building with thin walls and nosy neighbors. They had to go somewhere quiet, secluded. Earlier, at a gas station, he saw brochures for some cabins in the mountains. They were closed this time of year, but he wasn't above a little B and E.

"Time to take a little drive, Ms. Ryder."

He chuckled to himself, propping her up in his arms. To anyone passing, it would look like he was the sweet boyfriend carrying his sleeping lady to the car. He had a sedative there that would keep her knocked out 'til they got to the cabin.

This would work. He'd get the bitch lawyer to tell him where Kayla was, and then all his problems would disappear. Just like Kayla.

****

"Wake up bitch!"

The lawyer sucked in a sharp breath of air as he threw a cold glass of water in her face. She sputtered and coughed, eyes still closed

"I said, wake up!"

He raised his hand and brought it back down in a hard slap across her cheek. That forced her eyes open. She glanced up, eyes focusing on him, sitting in a chair across from her. The brown, frightened gaze darted around the cabin. She shifted and gasped when she realized she was bound with a thick rope to a kitchen chair. He was glad now he always kept some in his trunk for emergencies. She wiggled, testing the bindings, but he knew his stuff. No way would she break out of her bonds.

"Julie Ryder."

"David Tyler."

He smiled. So, she hadn't forgotten who he was. Sometimes knocking a person out could wipe a bit of their memory. "Oh good, you know who I am. That will make this so much easier."

"Make what easier?" She tested the ropes again. Such a pointless effort, but if she wanted to waste the energy, he wasn't going to stop her.

"I'm looking for someone, and I think you know where she is."

She stopped struggling, going still as a statue.

"Where's Kayla?"

"I don't know who you're talking about."

His smile slipped; the bitch was lying to him. He sighed, reaching under his chair and coming back up with a very sharp knife.

"I was hoping you'd be more agreeable, but I'm prepared to do this the hard way."

Gripping the weapon tightly, he let some of the rage burning inside him loose. In a flash he slashed out at her arm, right below her shoulder. Her scream soothed some of the fury swirling inside him as the razor sharp metal sliced into her skin, leaving a swath of red blood in its path.

"Now, I'll ask again. Where is Kayla?"

"I don't know." Tears swam in her eyes, but she didn't let them fall.

She was tougher than he expected, he'd give her that. "Really?" He struck out again, this time cutting her upper thigh.

She screamed again; he'd cut deeper, and this time, she didn't stop the flood of tears pouring down her cheeks.

He left his chair, coming around behind her. Leaning down, he whispered in her ear. "Now, listen to me carefully, Julie." He dragged the blade of the knife ever so softly against her throat. "I can be a reasonable man. Tell me where Kayla is and I'll let you go."

Fat chance. He couldn't leave any witnesses behind, but she didn't need to know that. People tended to believe anything when their life was on the line.

"If you insist on lying to me, well, I hate to be cliché, but I have ways of making you talk. If carving your flesh won't work…" He moved the knife down her throat until the tip caught in her silk blouse and twisted his wrist, flicking the blade downward until it cut her shirt clean through. The tattered pieces of fabric hung open, leaving her exposed. Reaching down with his other hand, he roughly grabbing one breast and squeezed. "I can think of other things to do with this sweet skin."

A whimper escaped her. He saw the wheels turn behind her eyes, gauging the possibility of her getting out of this alive and unharmed.

The chance was zero, but he'd let her believe otherwise if it got him what he wanted.

"Tell me what I want to know and this can all just be a bad dream."

He pressed the knife against her chest until the point drew blood. Her eyes shut tight, and he knew he'd won. Relishing her defeat, he waited as her head hung, lips parting, and the sweet words he'd been waiting for came out.

"Peak Town."

"What?"

"She's in Peak Town. At a…safe house."

He patted her on the chin with the bloody blade.

"There now. That wasn't so hard, was it?"

He rose, walking around to sit, once more, in the chair across from her. Anticipation thrumming through his body, he dug his cell phone out of his pocket.

"Time to make a call. What's the number, Julie."

Jaw clenched tight, she pressed her lips together. Bitch still thought she could defy him? Raising the knife again he brought it up under her chin, pressing until a small drop of blood pooled on the tip. Brown eyes widened with fear. A whimper escaped her as she rattled off a number. *That's better.*

He punched in the digits, eager to have this whole mess over with. Once he told Kayla he had her precious lawyer, the bitch would come running. Ms. Goody Two-Shoes Teacher wouldn't want anyone dying in her place. A chuckle rose within as he imagined Kayla running to him to sacrifice herself for someone else.

Another sob rose from the bound woman in front of him.

There will be no sacrifice, he thought with glee.

Because both women would be dying, and he would return home a hero.

Chapter 24

After a few fitful hours of tossing and turning, Kayla decided it was time to stop moping around feeling sorry for herself and get up. So she had fallen in love? Big deal. People did it all the time. Whether or not Ryder loved her was of no consequence. She would deal with that situation when it presented itself.

If it ever did.

For now, she would be thankful for the time she had with him. Speaking of thanks, she had some kindness to return. Ryder had taken her into his home, was helping her with her problems, and had pleasured her body and soul. The least she could do was clean the guy's house.

Grateful for an opportunity to give back a little of what he gave, she set to work. After a quick breakfast of cold cereal and hot coffee, she went through the house, systematically cleaning. She started with the bathrooms, scrubbing the mildew from every nook and cranny of the tubs and disinfecting every surface she could reach. Then she moved on to the kitchen. It was pretty clean, but she wiped everything down anyway, stacking her breakfast dishes in the full dishwasher and running it.

Lastly, she searched until she found Ryder's vacuum cleaner in one of the closets. She was thankful he had a one-story house; the vacuum was ancient and weighed a ton. It would have been quite a feat to drag that behemoth up a flight of stairs. Still, it felt good to be doing something as normal as cleaning. She wondered how long it would be before she could get back that everyday standard.

It took half an hour to vacuum through the three bedrooms, hallway, and living room. As she shut off the power and wound the cord, it took her a moment to realize what the shrill ringing was. The phone. Ryder mentioned once how everyone in Peak Town still had landlines because the cell service in the mountains could be spotty. Being from the city, she hadn't had a landline in years.

She reached for the cordless phone, a smile on her face. Ryder had promised to check in on her, so she answered with a cheery, "Hello?"

Quiet static filled the air before a dark voice came over the line. "Hello, Kayla. So nice to hear your voice again."

Her heart skipped a beat, and ice shot through her veins at the cold, familiar tone. Fear gripped every inch of her body, freezing her in place. "D-David? How did you find me?"

An evil chuckle came over the line. "Oh, I had a little help with that. Say hello to your lawyer, Julie."

Julie? Ryder's sister?

She heard him mutter something to someone in the background then a woman's cry. "Kayla, I'm sorry!"

"Shut up, bitch," David screamed in the background. Then he was back on the line. "If you don't want your new friend to end up like your old one, you'll come to meet me."

Friend? She'd never met the woman. Had he

discovered Julie looking into his files and assumed Kayla hired her?

Her hands shook in terror as she realized her worst fears had come to life.

"You thought I wouldn't be able to find you?" he continued with a hiss. "Your lawyer may have tucked you away in a safe house, but no place is safe from me."

A safe house? He must think Julie hid her. Then maybe he didn't know about Ryder. That was good. But he had Ryder's sister. That was bad.

"Come to this address in the next hour. Alone, or I kill the lawyer and add another murder to your dossier."

David was more of a monster than she ever realized. He rattled off the address. No doubt a secluded place where no one would hear her screams.

"Okay, I'll be there. Just don't hurt her."

No, no, no! This was the reason she should have kept running. She never wanted to put anyone else in danger, never wanted anyone else to suffer Jen's fate.

"Tick tock, Kayla. One hour, and come alone or she *will* die." He hung up, his final threat ringing in her head.

She held the phone to her ear until the dial tone beeped. It was a trap, she knew. David had no intention of letting either of them out of there alive. But she had to go. If there was any hope of rescuing Ryder's sister, she had to take that chance. She would not allow him to lose the last remaining member of his family due to her.

Dammit! This was the exact reason she had not wanted him involved. She knew something like this would happen. David was hurting people because of her.

It stops now.

Rushing to the kitchen, Kayla eyed the large knife block on the counter. She grabbed two small steak knives, shoving one in each of her boots. Next, she grabbed the large carving knife. David might search her, but there was no way she was going to meet him unarmed. She might die today, but damned if she wouldn't go down fighting.

She slipped the carving knife into the back of her jeans, covering it with her long undershirt. The blade poked her skin, slipping at the slightest movement. *What am I thinking?* She wasn't some action star vigilante with a fake movie prop. This thing was very real and very sharp. No way could she drive out to David with a large knife in the back of her pants. She'd slice her backside up for sure. Good thing she had a large winter coat.

Carefully pulling the weapon out, she slipped it into the inner pocket of her jacket. *Much better.* Her gaze caught on the meat cleaver with longing, but there was no way she could conceal something that big on her person. She would have to make do with the three knives she had.

Grabbing a pen and a piece of paper from the junk drawer, she scribbled out a quick note for Ryder. She contemplated calling him, it *was* his sister in danger, but she didn't want to take the risk of David killing Julie. No, she had to go alone. If she could distract David, maybe Julie could make a run for it. This was her mess, and she needed to fix it.

But there was one more problem—how to get there?

Ryder only had one car and he took it into work.

Her gaze shifted out the kitchen window to the horse stall. Wind Chaser moved lazily around the fenced in pen. *No, I need to get there in one piece.* If she rode the giant beast, she'd be liable to fall off and break her fool neck, and then where would Julie be?

Thankfully, Ryder had written down a few numbers for her on the fridge. She picked up the phone again and dialed. Maggie answered on the first ring.

"Hi. It's Kayla."

"Hey, you coming into the shop today?"

"Actually, that's what I'm calling about. I need a favor."

The baker's cheerful voice held an edge of caution. "Everything okay?"

No it wasn't, but if her plan worked, everything soon would be.

Chapter 25

After leaving Kayla in bed this morning, Ryder itched to call her and check in. The accident scene had been ugly. Even so, the whole time he was taking statements, his mind wandered back to his bed and the woman he left there. He hated to leave her, but had no choice. He had a job to do.

If it were up to him, all DUI's would lose their licenses permanently.

He turned the key, locking the door to the station's one small cell. The drunk inside lay on the hard wooden bench; his loud snores indicated the man was now sleeping it off. After the driver had been pulled from the car, the EMT's had looked him over. Not a scratch on the guy.

Couldn't say the same for the other car.

The EMT's at the scene said the woman suffered a broken arm and possible concussion. Thankfully, the children sleeping in the backseat were uninjured. All three had been passed out when the crash occurred, the youngest, seven months old, buckled tight in his car seat.

Ryder's blood still boiled at the memory of those wide, terrified eyes. When he arrived at the scene, the mother was being loaded into the ambulance, the baby was screaming, the three year-old was crying for her daddy, and the five-year old boy with dark red hair kept asking if his mommy was going to be okay.

Damn near broke his heart. The fear coming off the kids ramped up his own worry for Kayla. Never before had he wanted to wrap up a scene so quickly.

The bleary-eyed drunk was barely coherent. The guy couldn't speak, let alone drive. What the hell had he been thinking? He hadn't. Therein lied the problem. Bastard could have killed the entire family. Instead, he scared them for life. Never had he wanted to kick a man's ass more. Sometimes he hated the fact he was the sheriff and had to maintain the law, because beating up a drunkard, even if he deserved it, was not standard police protocol.

"Hey, Sheriff?"

Ryder turned from watching the drunk guy snore away to face Mrs. Billings.

"The hospital called. The woman has a broken ulna and a mild concussion. The kids are all medically fine, a little shaken up, but fine. The husband is there with them now. They were on their way to the airport to pick him up. Poor guy got a pretty terrible homecoming."

"At least they're all alive." Tremors shook his usually steady hands. Damn accident brought up memories of his own father's fatal collision with a drunk driver. Add that to his worry for Kayla and his nerves were shot to hell. "That's something to be thankful for."

Mrs. Billings nodded. "It is indeed. I also got word on Tim."

"How's he doing?"

"Couple of stitches, a tetanus shot, and he's right as rain."

"Have Jason go pick him up."

The older woman smiled. "Already done."

Of course it was. She was on top of everything. *Going to be tough to find her replacement once she retires.* The woman kept the place running like a well-oiled machine.

"Thank you, Mrs. Billings. I don't know what we would do without you."

She chuckled, waving a hand in the air. "Run around like a bunch of chickens with your heads cut off, I imagine."

A smile tugged at his lips. She wasn't too far off.

"Why don't you go grab something to eat, Sheriff? Green and Cummings are in. They can hold down the fort for a bit."

He glanced at the clock. *Holy cow, it's already eleven.* He'd been so busy handling everything, he hadn't noticed how late it was.

His stomach chose that moment to growl loudly, reminding him he hadn't eaten since dinner last night. Food and coffee would be good right about now. Lots of coffee.

His nerves were on edge also, anxious to check in on Kayla. He hadn't liked leaving her this morning. His hours could be wonky at times; emergencies came up, and he had to deal with them. She'd handled it like a champ when he told her he had to leave.

There had been a moment there when he almost confessed his feelings. He cared for Kayla, but it was more than that he realized in that moment—he loved her. Body and soul.

It sounded crazy, given the amount of time they had known each other, but he had no doubt she was the woman he had been waiting for his whole life. His father once told him he knew Ryder's mother was the other half of his soul the moment he met her.

That was how Ryder felt about Kayla.

She was so strong and independent, had to be because of how she'd grown up...alone. It broke his heart every time he thought about her childhood, being shuffled from house to house, never finding a home. Never having a family. Then she found Jen, a sister at heart, only to lose her in the most brutal way. Life wasn't fair sometimes.

How she managed to go through so much heartache and still come out such a kind, bright, caring person he would never know. But it was amazing. *She* was amazing. And he loved her without a single shred of doubt. She was the woman he wanted to spend the rest of his days with.

When he tried to convey his feelings this morning, however, he had seen uncertainty in her eyes. Whether she was unsure of her feelings or scared to take a leap of faith, he had no idea. He hoped it was the latter. Fear he could help her overcome, but if she didn't love him...well, that would mean a lifetime of loneliness for him. Kayla was the one for him. If she didn't feel the same, he would let her go...and his wasted heart would love her until the day he died.

"I'll be back in about an hour," he said to Mrs. Billings. "I have my cell on if anything comes up."

The station mom waved him away, assuring him she could handle things. More than once he found himself pondering if she was secretly Wonder Woman.

Ryder headed outside into the cold air. November kept getting colder and colder. He hoped they weren't in for a nasty winter. Snow was great for tourists, but freezing pipes were hell on townsfolk.

As he made his way down the steps of the small stationhouse, he heard someone call out. Looking up, he saw Maggie running straight toward him, her face pinched with worry.

His senses went on red alert. A million scenarios filled his brain—something was wrong with Lizzy and Dade's baby, the shop was in trouble again, someone at the ranch got thrown from a mount.

She stopped in front of him, cold air turning her breath to little white puffs of smoke.

"Maggie, what is it? What's wrong?"

Her gloved hands twisted. "I don't know. I mean, I'm not sure anything is wrong. Kayla called and asked to borrow my car."

Kayla? She was supposed to stay at home today. The red alert went nuclear. Why would she need a car? "Did she say why?"

The baker shook her head, small strands of hair falling from her French braid. "No. I picked her up about ten minutes ago from your house. She dropped me off back at the shop. She didn't say a thing the whole drive, just sat there with a determined look on her face, and, Ryder…she was scared. I could tell, but she wouldn't talk to me. She kept saying she had an errand to run and everything was fine." Her lower lip trembled. "I'm sorry. I should have contacted you the minute she called me. I can't help but think something is very wrong."

Neither could he. At the best, Kayla freaked and took off. At the worst, David found her. He needed answers. The first place to start looking was the last place she had been.

He gave her a brief hug, noticing the tears gathered in the corner of her eyes. "Thanks for telling me, Maggie. I'm sure everything is fine."

She squeezed him hard, pressing her face into his chest. Her voice muffled as she spoke, "You're as bad a liar as I am, Jake Ryder. I may not know everything, but I know that girl is running from something."

Yes, and he prayed it hadn't caught her.

Knowing time was precious, he ran to his truck, hitting the gas almost as soon as the engine turned over. His heart and mind raced at breakneck speed with worry.

He made it back to the house in record time. One step inside and he knew Kayla was gone. The air felt heavy, the house empty. He searched the rooms quickly, looking for a clue as to where she would have run and why.

All of her clothing still sat in the bedroom, so she hadn't gone away for good. His heart shuttered with relief. It was a pretty safe bet Kayla planned on returning. Then why had she needed Maggie's car? And why had she been so secretive?

A hinkey feeling settled deep in his gut. Something was off.

He made his way into the kitchen. Frenzy settling into a calm worry, he noticed the countertops were so clean they sparkled. Had Kayla cleaned his house? His frantic mind didn't even question the fact his house was cleaner than it had ever been, too focused on finding her to give it a second thought. Now, if only he knew where the fool woman was so he could thank her properly.

From the corner of his eye, something caught his

attention. There, on the perfectly polished counter, was a piece of paper. No, a note.

A note from Kayla explaining where she went? He hoped so.

Ryder snatched up the paper, his gaze rapidly moving over the elegantly written script.

Dear Ryder,

I'm so sorry. It seems my troubles have caught up with me. David somehow discovered your sister was helping me. It's all my fault. He took her.

His heart stopped. *Julie!* That monster had his baby sister.

He wants to do an exchange. Her for me. I know it's a trap, but maybe I can buy your sister some time to escape. I have to try. I am so, so sorry about everything. You are the most amazing man I have ever met. I never wanted to cause you any pain. I should have left the night you found me. I never should have brought my problems to your doorstep.

David is staying in a cabin just off Pine Ridge Road.

Ryder was familiar with the cabin, a rental property, but boarded up during the winter season. The perfect place to take a hostage. Kayla was an idiot to go there alone. David probably warned her not to tell the police or he would kill Julie, and sweet Kayla, who was so concerned for his sister's safety, complied with the dirty cop's demand.

But the note told him she knew he would come after her. She was following David's instructions, but making a backup plan of her own.

Smart woman.

Thank you for everything you've done for me.

These past two weeks with you have been the happiest of my life—except the whole being framed for murder thing of course.

He smiled at her ill attempt at humor.

I'll get her back for you. I promise. You won't have to lose another person you love.

Kayla

Silly woman, didn't she realize he loved *her*? Did she think sacrificing herself for his sister was really what he wanted?

Well, she had another thing coming, because he would not lose either of them. Not to a jackass like David Tyler. If that bastard hurt one hair on either Julie or Kayla's head, sheriff or not, Ryder would kill the guy. And damn the consequences. Tyler had the two most important women in his life. He would stop at nothing until they were both safely back in his arms.

Chapter 26

Cold wind whipped the short strands of Kayla's hair into her face. Reaching up, she pushed the hair behind her ear with frozen fingertips. She should have worn gloves, but proper winter attire had been the last thing on her mind. Hopefully, she wasn't too late. Julie had to be alive. There was no other acceptable scenario. The thought of Ryder losing another family member was unbearable. And to be the cause of it…that was too much.

Maggie's borrowed car sat in the driveway. The kind woman had been so worried, inquiring as to what was going on, but Kayla didn't dare tell her. The less people who knew, the better. Ryder and Julie were already dragged into her mess. She did not want to involve anyone else. This was her problem, and she would fix it.

A shiver, having nothing to do with the cold, raced down her spine.

She prayed Ryder got her note on time. David told her to come alone, and she had, but she wasn't an idiot. She knew there was no way he would let her or Julie walk away. He couldn't risk either of them talking. Kayla knew he intended to kill them both. That would not happen if she had anything to say about it. Ryder would come after his sister, no doubt in her mind. Now, all she had to do was make sure Julie stayed alive until he got here.

And if she had to sacrifice her own life for Julie's, so be it.

A terrified sob rose up in her throat. Hopefully, it wouldn't come to that.

Touching a hand to her jacket, she felt for the large carving knife securely held in the inside pocket. She knew she was bringing a knife to a gunfight, but it was better than no weapon at all.

Plucking up all the courage she could muster, she placed one foot in front of the other and continued toward the cabin. It looked like any other vacation property, small, one story, two aged, wooden rocking chairs sitting on the front porch. The whole scene was very quaint and picturesque; such an antithesis to the current situation, she almost laughed. From the outside, one would think this place the perfect retreat for a little tranquility. No one would ever guess a murderer lay in wait.

Taking a deep, fortifying breath, she made her way up the weatherworn stairs. They creaked under her footsteps. No matter. The element of surprise wasn't a part of her plan. David knew she was coming. He most likely heard the car pull up.

She didn't really have much of a plan, to be honest. Distract David so Julie could run, and hope Ryder showed up before David killed her. She bit her bottom lip. Not much of a plan, but it was all she had. She was a kindergarten teacher for goodness sake; her lesson plans included the ABC's and shape recognition. Dealing with a psychotic killer was out of her area of expertise.

Her body trembled as she reached the front door.

Foregoing a knock, she grabbed the knob and turned. The door swung open with ease, and Kayla stepped into the small cabin. Chilly air blasted her, freezing her to the bone, the temperature inside colder than the outdoors somehow. Her gaze fell upon a woman bound to a kitchen chair in the middle of the room. Her long, dark hair hung in a tangled mess around her face. Blood stained parts of the torn silk blouse.

Bile rose in Kayla's throat. *What had David done?*

She stepped tentatively into the room. "Julie?"

The woman's head slowly rose. The dark, chocolate eyes reminded her of Ryder. Yes, this had to be Julie Ryder; she would bet her life on it. A despondent laugh rose inside her as she realized she was doing just that.

"Kayla?" Her voice came out harsh and scratchy. The way one sounded after a bout of screaming.

She nodded, a tear slipping from her eye. "I'm so sorry, Julie. I never wanted to put you in any danger."

"Awe, now isn't that sweet." A vile chuckle came from behind her.

She spun around, coming face to face with the man she feared most.

David Tyler looked...disheveled. Not as polished as usual. Chasing down a witness while trying to cover up a murder must do that to a man.

"Don't you know, Kayla," he continued, "*you* are danger. A dangerous murderer on the run, willing to kill anyone who gets in her way."

"David, how did you find me?"

"I have my ways." He nodded to the bound Julie. "One of my contacts alerted me the minute your lawyer started digging into my past. It wasn't hard to track her down." His eyes gleamed. "And it wasn't hard to break her down."

A muffled sob came from the bound woman. Her heart broke. What had David done to her? Torture?

The bastard!

"I'm here now. So you can let her go."

He laughed, almost doubling over. "Oh, Kayla. Are you really that stupid?"

No, she wasn't, but she wanted to give him the opportunity to keep his word. Silly her.

"I can't let her go. I can't let either of you go. You know that."

She nodded, the last thread of hope inside her breaking. She did know.

"No, no. Neither of you is leaving here alive. A nice little accident will take care of this whole mess, don't you think?"

No she did not. But he wasn't really asking her opinion.

"So, how is this going to go down, David? What's the story this time?" Because he had one, it was clear now he always had a story ready—and she needed to buy as much time as possible.

His lips twisted in a cruel smile, making her skin crawl. How had he hid this evil for so long? He'd always given her a bad vibe, but she never would have pegged him as a murderer.

"I followed a lead to Colorado," he said, spinning his yarn. "Got a tip you were hiding out here. You found some poor, gullible lawyer to believe your innocent sob story."

His gaze darted to Julie. Dark eyes glared. Kayla took heart seeing the fire in the other woman's gaze.

206

She hadn't given up yet.

Good, perhaps we have a chance.

"I came out here to apprehend you, but sadly, before I could, tragedy struck."

Doesn't it always.

David shook his head, looking crestfallen. The man really missed a career in Hollywood.

"On your way into town, your car hit a patch of ice, swerved off the road, and fell down the side of the mountain. Both you and your lawyer friend died in a fiery crash before I could get to you."

The glee in his voice belied the regretful look in his eyes. He'd have to work on that for the cameras.

"A car accident, David? Really? That's the worst set up I've ever heard. Surely, you can do better than that."

His gaze narrowed, lips curling back in a snarl.

Never had she been more terrified in her life, but she couldn't let him see that. Affecting a bored tone, mustering up all the false bravado she had, she added, "I mean, how are you going to get us in the car? You don't think we'll willingly drive to our deaths do you?"

He reached into his jacket pocket. When his hand emerged, it held a black handgun.

Breath catching in her lungs, she held back a gasp of terror. She expected he would have one, but reality was still a shock. Her heart jumped into her throat, and she began to reevaluate her hastily made plan.

He motioned with the gun. "Go untie her. And don't get any ideas. Any funny business and I'll blow both of your brains away."

"Kind of hard to make *that* look like an accident." She was proud that her voice came out strong, because inside, she shook so hard it felt as if she would shatter.

"You'd be surprised what a plunge off a fifty foot cliff can hide."

She shuddered, picturing the fall in her mind. The road on the way to the cabin contained many a blind curve—tall drops with no guardrail, just a straight plunge down the mountainside to the hard, rocky ground below. Any number of them would be perfect for the scenario he laid out. She had to make her move before getting into the car; once they were in the vehicle, it would be too late.

Keeping David in her sights, she made her way over to Julie, knelt behind the chair, and went to work on the tightly knotted ropes. David watched her with a sharp eye, bringing the muzzle of the gun up, taking aim directly at her head. At a distance of a few feet there was little chance he would miss.

"Julie," she whispered softly. "I have a plan." *Sort of.* "Ryder is on his way." *I hope.*

"Jake?" The woman's voice cracked on her brother's name.

"I'll distract David. When I do, you run. Run as fast as you can." Maggie's car still sat in the driveway, but Julie wouldn't have time to hop in and start the engine. Taking off on foot using the cover of the trees would be the fastest way to escape.

"What about you?"

"Don't worry about me. I'll be fine." A lie. Between a knife and a gun, she knew which would win. But if she could give the woman a head start she would. Julie had to live, not only for Ryder, but also so she could tell the world about David, and who he really was.

Gaze on the madman with the gun, Kayla slipped the knife from her left boot into Julie's hand. In case she didn't make it and David came after Julie, she wanted the woman to have a way to defend herself. Again, it wasn't much, but it was better than nothing.

"When I say run, you *run*. Got it?"

The dark head nodded ever so slightly.

"Hurry it up." David scowled, his grip tightening on his weapon.

"I'm trying. These knots are tight."

She undid the last of the ropes binding Julie. Ryder's sister held the knife tightly in her grip. Kayla pulled the lawyer's sleeve over her hand so the blade didn't show, then helped her stand. Julie faltered, her knees giving way. Kayla caught her.

Oh no, what if she's too weak to run? She couldn't fight off David and protect Julie at the same time.

"We knock him over. Get the gun out of his hands. Then we *both* run," Julie whispered in her ear.

Holy cow! The woman wasn't weak, she was strategizing. She didn't know why she was surprised. It made sense the woman had a backbone of steel and a cool head in a crisis. Just like her brother.

Kayla sent up another silent prayer that Ryder had gotten her note and was on his way up the mountain. "Okay, you go low. I'll go high."

"Stop whimpering to each other and let's go," David complained.

"I was just apologizing again for getting her into this." She held Julie as if the other woman needed the support to stand. Together, like a choreographed dance, they stepped closer to David.

"Yeah, too bad Julie here didn't know what

happens to people around you. Right, Kayla?" His lip curled with nastiness. "Daddy didn't want you, mommy threw you away, best friend murdered—"

"*You* killed her, you bastard!"

"Yes, but everyone thinks it was you. People don't last long around you, do they, Kayla? If I believed in them, I'd say you were cursed."

That was enough. She couldn't stand there and listen to another second of this pompous, crazy murderer's tirade. The time had come to take David Tyler down.

Literally.

Moving with Julie, she whispered with each step, "One...two...*now*."

She pounced, and Julie dove, taking out David's legs. Kayla aimed for the gun, slamming her clasped hand into David's wrist. Taken by surprise, he shouted, falling to the ground. The gun flew from his grasp, sliding across the floor.

"Run!" she screamed. Grasping the other woman by the arm, she dragged her up, bolting out the door and flying down the front steps.

They were going to make it! They were going to be—

A shot rang out in the air, and a stab of cold, sharp, pain struck her right calf. She tumbled to the ground, face slamming into the snow and dirt.

"Kayla!" Julie screamed, stopping to help.

Another shot rang out. The snow near Julie flew up into the air. The poor, terrified woman screamed again, covering her head with her hands. She glanced up, her face whiter than the snow surrounding them. Kayla looked behind her to see David standing on the front porch, gun back in hand, the knife she'd given Julie sticking out of his left thigh.

She hadn't even seen the woman pull it out. Julie Ryder was good. Just like her brother.

David took a step and his injured leg gave out, causing him to stumble and grab for the porch railing.

Grasping the opportunity, she pushed at Julie. "No, run. Keep going. Get Ryder. Please, you have to *run!*"

The woman's forehead wrinkled with indecision. Worry filled her gaze. She knew Julie didn't want to leave, but she had to. She had to run or they would both be dead.

"Julie, *go!*"

"I'll get Ryder. We'll come back for you," she promised. "Just hold on."

Kayla nodded, and grabbed a rock the size of her palm. Sitting up, she lobbed it as hard as she could at David's head. "Go!"

The murderous bastard ducked the flying rock, but it served its purpose. It distracted him while Julie made her escape as fast as she could down the road. Now, Kayla just had to survive until help arrived.

He stormed toward her, a crazed look in his dark eyes. The gun never wavered in his grip, knife in the thigh barely slowing him as rage, pure and hot, fueled his every step.

Fear like she had never known poured like ice water through every inch of her being as she fisted her hand around another large rock.

Please, Ryder. Hurry!

Chapter 27

Ryder cursed the icy roads forcing him to drive with more caution than he had time for, but he wouldn't be much good to Julie or Kayla if he drove off the side of the mountain.

The cabin was up ahead, only a few minutes away. When he came around the next bend he would be able to see it. His heart beat furiously in his chest.

Please be okay. Please be okay. Please be okay.

The mantra repeated in his head. He had no idea what he would do if he lost his sister or Kayla. Life would be a hell of a lot darker, for sure.

As he carefully guided his car around the next curve, he saw a figure in the middle of the road. A woman, running full force, straight toward him. He tapped the brakes to avoid fishtailing on the slick, ice-covered road, turning the car onto the shoulder to avoid her. As she got closer, recognition hit him full force.

"Julie!" He threw open the car door, screaming his baby sister's name again as he ran to meet her.

"Jake! *Ohmigod, Jake!*"

Julie launched herself into his arms. Tears streamed down her face. Her body shook. He held her close, thanking everything in the universe his baby sister was once again safe in his arms.

But as happy as he was to see her safe, his brain recognized she was alone.

Pulling back gently, he glanced down at her. "Julie, where's Kayla?"

She choked back a sob as her arm rose to point behind her. The motion drew his attention to the blood on her clothes. He did a quick visual scan of the slashes on her arms and legs.

A dark cloud of rage rose inside. *I am going to kill David Tyler.*

"Shit, Julie. What did that monster do to you? Are you all right?"

She waved his concern away, breath coming in short pants. "I'm fine. K-Kayla is still back there. Made me run. T-told me to get help." His baby sister was frantic, practically screaming now. "Jake, she's back there with h-him. He's going to kill her!"

Every cell in his body froze. His heart, his brain, everything stopped functioning for a split second. Then a gunshot rang out in the air and his mind snapped.

"Get in the car," he ordered his sister. "Use the radio to call the station. I already have back up on the way. Tell them everything that's going on."

She nodded, sniffing back tears. Bloodied arms wrapped around his neck, embracing him tightly. "Be careful, big brother."

Then she ran toward his still running truck. Ryder checked his police issued gun, full clip and two extras on his belt. Knowing he would need the element of surprise, he eschewed the road for the dense tree cover. He would come up on the side of the cabin instead of heading straight toward it. Hopefully, it would give him an advantage.

Images of Julie's marred, bleeding flesh rose in his mind, and he had to fight back the urge to howl with rage. David Tyler had signed his death warrant when he hurt his baby sister. If one inch of Kayla's smooth, creamy flesh was even bruised, the monster was going to find out how wild the west could be.

****

Kayla rolled to her side, army crawling behind a large snow dusted boulder. More shots rang out in the air. She held in a scream as the snow, inches from her feet, sprayed into the air with the impact of a bullet.

"Oh dear." David's dark chuckle filled the quiet mountain air. "That one came a bit close didn't it? Do you know how many times a person can be shot before they die, Kayla? You'd be surprised. You're going to look like Swiss cheese before I'm done with you."

His shots were getting closer. The psycho was toying with her, ramping up her fear before going in for the kill. How long did she have before he tired of this cat and mouse game?

At least Julie is safe.

The one thing she could take solace in. The one thing she knew she did right. She may have failed Jen, but Julie got away. Ryder would not lose his little sister. If nothing else, that was enough.

But she would really prefer it if she lived, too.

Another two shots cracked through the stillness of the snowy forest. The rock she hid behind was large, but she heard the bullets smack into its broad face, fracturing bits of stone off the large boulder.

"You can't hide forever, Kayla," David's manic voice shouted into the wind.

True, and with her leg currently going numb, she doubted she could run either. Pulling her pant leg up, she saw a huge chunk of skin missing at the top of her calf. Blood flowed out of the wound. She needed to apply pressure or risk passing out soon. Then she'd be a sitting duck.

Pulling the yellow knit cap from her head, she pressed it against the wound as hard as she could, suppressing a scream as pain shot like fire through her leg. Using her other hand, she quickly undid her belt, pulling it from her pant loops and wrapping it around her leg and the hat. She pulled the belt as tight as she could then fastened the buckle. Crude, but it would have to do for now. Tears of pain and anguish poured down her face, but she wiped them away.

Daring a glance, she peeked out over the side of the boulder. David slowly made his way toward her hiding spot. Blood poured out his nose. The second rock she had lobbed at him in her attempt to get away made direct contact with his nose. By the swollen look of it, she most likely broke it.

Score one for me.

He limped as he made his way toward her, the knife she had given Julie still sticking out of his thigh. It must have hit something important, because it appeared to be slowing him down quite a bit. Good. She needed every advantage she could get if she was going to get out of this alive. And she damn well planned to.

"Going to be pretty hard to cover this up, David," she taunted. "Hard to make it look like a car accident if I'm full of bullet holes."

"Shut up, bitch!" He raised the gun and fired.

She ducked back behind the rock. *Good.* If she could get him to waste all his ammunition, then she could try to run without the risk of flying bullets coming toward her. But when she attempted to stand, her right leg immediately gave out, sending her crashing back onto the hard, snow-packed ground.

Biting her cheek, she held in a scream of pain. *Okay, plan B.*

Kayla reached into her jacket pocket and pulled the large carving knife free. If she couldn't run, she would attack. As long as David's gun was empty, she had a chance.

Time to poke the beast.

"You know," she called out. "I'm not surprised you caught Jen talking to other men. She was probably shopping around for a new guy. Yeah, she said you had some bedroom issues. What did she call it…oh, right— the fastest five seconds *ever*." Jen had said no such thing, but she needed him irrationally angry. The best way to make a man like him livid was to insult his bedroom skills.

It worked. David let out a howl of rage. She counted as five more cracks of gunfire pierced the air.

That was, what? Ten shots? Eleven? How many rounds are in his gun?

She had no idea. There was also the possibility he had extra clips. She prayed he didn't.

"Julie is going to tell everyone about you." She hoped the woman had gotten to safety. "Everyone will know you're a murderer. Even if you kill me, you're not going to get away with it."

"I'll deal with that lawyer bitch once I finish with you. Besides, my family has enough money and power to make anything go away. Not that you would know anything about power *or* family, Kayla."

He had to keep hitting that sore spot, didn't he?

"No one is going to miss *you* when you're gone."

"Wanna bet, asshole?"

As she recognized that deep, sexy voice, Kayla cried in relief, heart pounding against her chest. Peeking out from behind the boulder, she saw the most beautiful sight she had ever laid eyes on.

Ryder—decked out in his sheriff uniform looking every bit the warrior he was—stood ten feet to the right side of David, gun aimed right at his chest.

The bad cop whirled around with his own gun, dropping it slightly when he saw whom he was facing. "Oh, Sheriff, thank God you're here." His voice seamlessly changed from madman to concerned citizen. "My name is David Tyler. I'm a police officer from Chicago, and I've been following the trail of a fugitive. She's wanted for murder back in Illinois—"

"I know who you are," Ryder interrupted coldly. "Put your weapon down and put your hands behind your head."

"Sheriff, you don't seem to understand. I'm trying to catch a killer."

"No, *you* don't seem to understand." He slowly inched closer. "I know who you are and what you did. And as much as I'd like to kill you for hurting the women I love, it's going to be much more satisfactory to see you rot in a cell for the rest of your life, you pathetic dick."

Kayla watched the exchange, her heart beating so loud she was sure they could hear it. Grabbing the large rock beside her, she pulled herself up against it, putting all her weight on her uninjured leg.

"I don't understand?" David shook his head, still trying to play innocent.

He did it quite well, she had to admit. *Bastard.*

"Read the badge, asshole. Sheriff Jake *Ryder*."

The crooked cop's eyes went wide.

"Yeah, the woman you abducted and tortured? That's my baby sister. And I'm going to make you pay for every bit of pain you caused her."

She watched as David's demeanor changed again. His jaw clenched, gaze narrowed. The hand holding his gun began to rise until it pointed straight at Ryder.

"Looks like I have a bigger mess to clean up than I thought. No matter, since it is obvious you were in on it with your sister, helping Kayla. I can spin this my way. Make you look like a dirty cop."

"The only dirty cop here is you, Tyler."

The vile man laughed, the maniacal sound bouncing off the snow covered trees, echoing in the still mountain forest. "Yeah, but no one is ever going to know that, will they? Shall we see who the fastest draw in the west is, Sheriff?" David mocked as he took aim.

Fear grabbed a tight hold on Kayla. At such close range, David would kill Ryder for sure. She couldn't have saved Julie only to lose Ryder. He saved her, in every way imaginable, and she loved him with her entire being.

Without thought to her injured leg, she launched herself out from behind the boulder. Knife in hand, she screamed, plunging the blade deep into the back of the bastard who killed her friend and tried to ruin her life.

The moment she struck, his gun went off. He howled in pain, reaching for his back, his weapon slipping from his grip. Swinging around, he smacked her in the head with his fist. Blinding pain burst through her skull. She went down, pulling him with her. They fell in a sprawl of arms and legs.

She could hear Ryder shouting in the background. Was he hit? Was he bleeding, dying? She wanted to check, but her main focus was on David, who was currently pinning her to the ground. Her leg burned, head pounded, vision blurred, but she had to push through it. David would not beat her. Kicking and punching with all her might, she tried to dislodge him, but he was bigger and stronger.

"You stupid bitch," he screamed, spittle flying from the corner of his mouth to land on her face. "You ruined everything!"

"No, *you* did." Tears freezing as they fell from her eyes, she used every bit of strength in her to kick, scratch, and maim any part of this evil monster she could reach. "When you killed the sweetest, kindest, most wonderful woman in the whole wide world."

"Oh, spare me your sisterhood solidarity."

Still struggling under his brutal grip, she managed to free her right arm. She slipped her hand down into her blood and snow soaked boot and felt around until her fingertips hit the hilt of the other steak knife she had stashed there.

"Spare this," she muttered, pulling the knife free and driving it hard and fast into his stomach.

His dark, cold eyes went wide with shock. He sucked in a sharp breath and collapsed on top of her, heavy, suffocating.

Then suddenly, David's body lifted away, and she was engulfed in warm, strong arms, and a deep woodsy scent.

"Kayla, sweetheart. Are you all right?"

Ryder! He was okay. He wasn't dead…and neither was she. The best possible outcome had come true.

"I'm okay. I'm okay."

Ryder pulled back, his concerned gaze going over every inch of her. Blood poured from his head, and he swiped at it to keep it from going into his eyes.

"You're hurt!"

"Just a graze." He squeezed her tightly again, as if assuring himself she was indeed unharmed. "It just knocked me on my ass for a moment. Head wounds bleed, but it's not that bad, baby. I promise."

A shuttered moan came from the body lying on its side in the snow. She squelched a scream as Ryder placed his body in front of hers, bringing his gun up on David's prone form. Reaching out with a gloveless hand, he felt for a pulse.

"Is he alive?" she asked quietly.

"Unfortunately." He shook his head with disgust. Sirens wailed in the distance. "Sounds like back up is on its way, so he'll probably make it."

He leaned down to the still living man's ear. "But I promise you, asshole, you will never see the outside of a prison cell ever again. I'm making it my personal mission to see you pay for every single one of your crimes. It's dirt bags like you that give cops a bad name. Bet the guys in lock up are going to love getting their hands on a crooked cop."

Kayla thought she heard David whimper but felt no pity for him. He had threatened, tortured, and killed people she loved. She heard stories about what inmates did to cops in prison.

David Tyler deserved everything he was about to get.

Lights flashed, reflecting off the white, powdery snow dotted red with blood. An ambulance and three cop cars pulled into the driveway of the cabin.

"Over here," Ryder called to his officers.

For the first time since she got that awful phone call this morning, Kayla's heartbeat settled to a normal rhythm. It was over. David was caught red-handed. Everyone would know exactly what kind of monster he was. It wouldn't be hard to prove her story now.

A sob of relief escaped her, and she buried her face in Ryder's chest.

"Come on, sweetheart." Strong arms pulled her up into his comforting hold. "Let's get you looked at, and then we can go home."

Home. It sounded so nice.

But a sad, sinking feeling entered her chest. Now that everything was over, now that she wasn't running anymore, the real question was, where *was* her home?

Chapter 28

Ryder sat on the hard plastic hospital chair. Edgy energy still coursed through his body. He'd wanted to kill that bastard Tyler. Almost had. There was a moment when the jerk was lying on the ground, bleeding, struggling to breathe, Ryder had entertained serious thoughts of murder. It would have been so easy to place his hand on the man's neck and twist. Hell, the guy was almost dead anyway.

The only thing that stopped him was the look in Kayla's eyes. She looked at him like he was a hero, a frickin' white knight or something. He was no hero, just a man doing his job. But some small part of him didn't want the hero worship in her gaze to go away. He didn't want to let her down like so many in her life had before.

So, I let the bastard live.

Now, here he was, in the county hospital, waiting to hear the conditions on the two most important people in his world. The ambulance only had room for one patient, and since David Tyler had been most in need, the asshole had gotten the ride. Ryder had tucked his sister and Kayla in the back of a squad car driven by his deputy. The green cop drove them all to county while the others processed the scene.

After arguing with the doctors and nurses, he relented his demand to go with his sister and Kayla when they arrived at the hospital. A young doctor, so small a strong breeze looked like it would knock her over, pointed out he couldn't go with both women seeing as how they would be receiving different care. She also—quite forcefully for her size—pushed him onto an exam bed and informed him, sheriff or not, his butt could not leave the spot until she had a look at his head wound.

After a short examination, the doc concluded it to be a bullet graze, nothing serious. He could have told her that. Five stitches, a shot of antibiotics, and he was right as rain. Except for the worrying knot in his gut that he knew wouldn't go away until he saw Julie and Kayla.

The stale cup of coffee he purchased half an hour ago sat untouched on the table next to him. Nerves on high alert, he darted his gaze all around the place, waiting for someone to bring him news, an update, anything.

A surgeon, hair graying at the temples and thin lines bracketing his mouth, came down the hallway. His soft shoes made no noise on the hard tiled floor. If he hadn't been scanning his surrounds, Ryder wouldn't have even noticed the doctor's approach. He rose to meet him, wondering who he was about to get news on.

"Sheriff Ryder?"

"Yes." Sweat coated his palms, and he wiped them on his jeans.

"I'm Doctor Krum. I have the status report on your suspect."

Tyler, dammit! He didn't give a shit about the man. He wanted to know about the women.

"The knife wounds to the shoulder and thigh damaged some muscle tissue, but they should heal in a few months with no long term damage."

Bully for the bastard.

"The wound to the stomach is a bit more severe. The blade punctured the intestine. We were able to repair the damage, but there may be some long-term effects. It's too early to tell."

David Tyler was alive and would stand trial. That was all that mattered. Any lasting injuries were just cause and well deserved.

But Ryder didn't care about that now. He had more pressing matters on his mind. "What about the two women I came in with? Julie Ryder and Kayla Jenkins?"

The doctor turned to the nurses' station and murmured something to the young man sitting in front of a computer. The nurse dug through a stack of files on the desk beside him. He pulled up two gray, metal clipboards and handed them to the doctor.

Krum glanced at the notes before responding to Ryder's query. "It seems Ms. Ryder—"

"My sister," he filled in unnecessarily.

The doctor gave him a sympathetic smile. "Your sister is going to be fine, Sheriff. She had some small knife wounds. None were deep enough to cause any real concern, but they did require stitches. The scarring should be minimal. The nurse gave her some painkillers and a tetanus shot. She's in room 107 if you would like to see her."

He nodded gratefully, one weight off his chest. "And Kayla?"

The doctor glanced at the other clipboard. "Ms. Jenkins is in surgery to repair a gunshot wound to her right calf. The bullet appears to have grazed her leg, tearing off skin and muscle. Thankfully, it did not hit any major arteries. She lost some blood, but the makeshift tourniquet she had on when she arrived stemmed the flow. A few days of bed rest and she'll be just fine." Dr. Krum looked up, green eyes serious. "She's very lucky."

No, she was very smart. *Smart as hell.* He was so damn proud of her. Most people would break down in a crisis, not Kayla. She pulled herself together and used her brains to save herself...and him.

Damn, he loved her so freaking much.

"As soon as she's transferred to a room, I will have a nurse inform you."

"Thank you, Doctor."

The older man inclined his head, handed the clipboards back to the nurse, and headed down the hallway. At that moment, Ryder's cell rang. The nurse gave him a stern look and pointed to a sign indicating no cell phone use. Too relieved to argue with the man, he held up a hand in apology and walked down the hall toward room 107.

Once he was out of sight of the cranky nurse, he dug his phone out of his pocket and answered. "Ryder."

"Hey, man, I've got some news for you."

Liam. "Give it to me."

"I was digging around in Tyler's files. Seems a few people who he should have put in jail are out walking the streets."

Imagine that.

"Let me guess," he said dryly. "They got off on technicalities?"

"Got it in one," Liam replied. "Somehow, evidence got 'misplaced' and the creeps walked. Tyler's not as good as he thinks he is. There's a paper trail linking him to some pretty nasty shit. Bribery, evidence tampering, and a whole host of seedy crap. And that's not all."

Of course it wasn't. David Tyler was a monster. No telling what depths of depravity this man went to.

"Tell me." He gripped his phone tightly.

"When I was digging, I noticed a few buried reports against Tyler. As if they were paid to disappear."

"Nothing disappears."

"Got that right, man. Anyway, it seems Tyler has a little problem keeping his hands off his lady friends. I tracked down two of the women, and they're willing to testify that David assaulted them, then threatened their lives if they ever spoke about it."

He was rethinking his decision to let Tyler live. The man was a devil who didn't deserve the air he breathed. The only solace Ryder had was, between today and everything Liam found, they could put Tyler away for the rest of his miserable life.

"I sent a copy of my report to Tyler's chief, and my boss gave me the clear to take him in, since some of this stuff crosses state lines. Now, I have to find the bastard."

"No need. I know exactly where he is."

Ryder proceeded to tell Liam the events of the day, skipping his inner battle with the value of letting Tyler live.

When he finished, his friend swore. "That sonofabitch! Is Julie okay?"

Liam had known Julie since the police academy days. The two of them had always been friendly, but from the worried tone in his buddy's voice, Ryder wondered just how friendly his best friend and little sister were.

"She's going to be fine. Some stitches and light scarring is all."

"Shit, man. How are you holding up?"

By a thread.

"Fine."

Liam chuckled. "Yeah, sure you are. Sit tight, buddy. I can be there in a few hours. I've got a nice pair of shiny metal handcuffs for Tyler, and I'm itching to use them."

The phone disconnected, and Ryder smiled. He'd known his friend would come through for him. By this time tomorrow, Tyler would be recovering in the prison infirmary.

He smiled to himself as he pushed open the door to his sister's room. It was like any other hospital room, small, sterile, depressing. For one brief moment, he had a flashback to his mother's last moments...in a room similar to this one. He shook his head, clearing the image. Julie was fine. No one was dying here today.

"Hey, kiddo. How ya feeling?" He slowly approached the large, mechanical bed.

Julie smiled, her eyes slightly glazed. Painkillers he guessed.

"Jake, you're here."

"Where else would I be, brat?" He ruffled her hair playfully when all he really wanted to do was hold her close and never let anything bad happen to her ever again. But that was impossible, and he knew it.

Tears gathered in her dark brown eyes. "Oh, Jake. I was so scared."

Sitting on the edge of the bed and being mindful of her injuries, he gently gathered her in his arm. He could tell she was shaken up—his baby sister rarely cried in front of him.

"I'm so sorry. When David took me, I knew he would never let me go. But that's no excuse, I should have fought harder or done something. I didn't mean to tell David where Kayla was. I tried to be stronger, I just—"

"Hey, hey, hey," he interrupted, pulling back to look at her. "You did *nothing* wrong, Julie. You hear me? David Tyler is a monster who gets off on hurting people. The guy would have found Kayla with or without you. It's *my* fault for dragging you into this mess. I never should have involved you."

She shook her head. "It's what we do, big brother. Put the bad guys away. You catch them, and I lock them up."

"Yeah, but this time, the bad guy caught you. I could have lost you, Julie. Do you know what that would have done to me?" He pressed her face into his chest, fear forming a tight lump in his throat at the thought of losing the only family he had left. "I can't lose you, Julie. I won't."

She laughed, hiccupping as the tears fell. "Well, same goes to you. I can't lose you either. What's a girl to do without her big brother?"

If it were up to him, she wouldn't ever have to know. Never before in his life had he been so afraid. The fear had been a living thing, wrapping around him, squeezing the life out of him until he could see his sister and Kayla again. He knew he wasn't invincible and life often threw curve balls, but if it were up to him, neither Julie nor Kayla would ever know another moment of pain or fear in their lives.

Chapter 29

Kayla tugged on the scratchy hospital gown. Once she was released she would need something else to wear. Her clothes were trashed and also with the FBI as evidence. A heavy sigh left her. It was finally over.

Mixed emotions roiled in her gut. Happiness that Jen's killer was going to jail for a long, long time, sadness because her best friend was still dead, and confusion over what to do next. She realized she couldn't go back to Chicago. There was no way she could ever live in her apartment again. David had wiped away all the good memories with one horrible one; they were just too much to bear.

She contemplated staying in Peak Town, with Ryder. But last night, after she had been placed in a room, Ryder and Julie came to see her. She had been exhausted and on medication that made her sleepy, but she did hear snippets of conversation. She also saw— through hazy vision—the two siblings had been embracing each other so tightly, as if they were afraid to let go for fear of losing one another. Given their past losses, she could understand. Always wanting, but never having any family herself, Kayla envied the moment.

She was the reason Julie and Ryder almost had to say goodbye forever. If it wasn't for her, they never would have been in this mess. The poor young woman would now have to carry scars with her for the rest of her life...*because of me*. Ryder was almost killed, his sister was marked forever, and it was all her fault.

Her heart squeezed in her chest, shattering into a million pieces. No way could she stay here now. David had been right about one thing. She was cursed. Her parents had the right idea in abandoning her. She only brought misery and pain into the lives of those she loved.

Before he left her room, Ryder had bent down and placed a soft kiss on her forehead, whispering he would be back the next day. He might, but she wouldn't. Shame choked her with the thought of facing him again. Guilt hung like a heavy storm cloud over her head. She was no longer in trouble now that David had been arrested. Kayla didn't needed Ryder's protection. And he didn't need her. No one ever did.

Pain lanced through her. How could someone hurt so much and still breathe?

Her heart broke at the thought of leaving Ryder, but she didn't dare stay. The best thing for everyone would be for her to go. Move on. On to what, she had no idea, but she'd figure it out. As much as she wanted to stay here in Peak Town with her new friends and the man who held her heart, she knew she couldn't. Every time Ryder looked at her he would be reminded of how she almost cost him his sister. He would come to hate her.

That was the one thing she wouldn't survive.

"Well, you seem to be doing better this morning." A cheery looking nurse with golden blonde hair entered the room. "The doctor has given you the all clear. He's sending you home with some pain killers and wants you to stay off that leg for about a week."

No problem. She could stay at home and relax…as soon as she knew where home was. It wasn't Ryder's house, and she could never go back to the apartment she shared with Jen. So, where did that leave her?

"Do you need me to call someone to pick you up or do you have a ride coming?"

"Actually, would it be too much trouble to ask you to call me a cab to the bus station?"

The sugary smile died. "A cab? Oh sweetie, I don't think the doctor wants you to go home if no one is there to take care of you. Don't you have anyone you can call?"

Tears gathered in the corner of her eyes and she swallowed a sob. "No, there's no one." *Story of my life.*

The nurse worried her lip. Would they not release her unless someone came to get her? She couldn't risk being here when Ryder eventually showed up. If she saw him, she didn't think she'd have the courage to leave. And she needed to go, for his sake.

"I-I mean no one is here yet. My mother is flying in to take care of me, but her flight doesn't land for another hour. I'd really like to get home before that. Hospitals kind of scare me." The lie rolled easily off her tongue. A first for her.

The nurse's worried gaze melted into one of understanding. "You're not alone there, sweetie. I know a lot of people feel better in their own beds." She wrinkled her nose. "I think it's the smell of antiseptic. Kind of gets to you if you're not used to it. I'll contact City Cabs. They have the best drivers. I'll also rustle you up some scrubs since the police took your clothes. Can't have you leaving in that breezy gown now can we?" She stepped away, giving an encouraging smile over her shoulder as she opened the door. "Don't worry, sweetie. You'll be home before your mom lands."

Of course she would, because she had no mother, and no home.

At least I'm alive.

Kayla closed her eyes on a heavy sigh, and Ryder's warm, dark chocolate eyes filled her mind's vision. Unable to hold back any longer, she let the tears flow. Tears for a man too good for her. Tears for what could have been. Tears because, yes, she was alive, but what kind of life was she going to have without the man she loved?

Chapter 30

Ryder downed the last sip of coffee, placing his mug in the kitchen sink. He was anxious to get to the hospital and see Kayla, but he needed a morning caffeine boost first. Exhaustion was catching up to him after the chaotic events of yesterday and a long restless night.

He glanced over to the kitchen table where Julie and Liam were playing a very heated card game.

"You're cheating again."

"Am not."

"You can't play more than one card."

"Yes I can. It's called match, play, match. It's a house rule. Jake, tell him!"

His sister had instilled Ryder house rules. Zeros switched hands, you could match a draw two, causing your opponent to draw four, and most importantly, you could get rid of a lot of cards with matching numbers and then playing another card and playing a match on that one. Match, play, match. It was a thing. In his household anyway.

"She's right, man." He grinned at the miffed look on Liam's face. The guy did not like to lose. Ever.

"See." She stuck her tongue out at the disgruntled FBI agent.

Liam grumbled, pulling a card from the top of the deck. "It's a stupid rule, and if you weren't recovering,

I'd argue you on it."

Julie grinned in triumph. She liked to win, too. It was one of her strongest assets in the courtroom.

Seeing the two had everything under control, he grabbed his keys, the pull to be at Kayla's side insistent.

"You guys going to be okay if I leave for a little bit?"

"For the last time, big brother, we'll be fine."

"It's just that I promised Kayla I'd be there before she woke up, and I'm running later than I expected. Chief Vic kept me on the phone longer than I anticipated and—"

"Ryder, it's fine, man." Liam's face held a serious note, a promise in his gaze. "I'll keep her safe."

He knew it was over. David was locked up. His sister was safe. Still, seeing her in the hospital last night, bruised and bandaged, kept his fear churning at the forefront of his mind.

"Yeah, I'm fine, big brother. Now, go get your woman so I can thank her for saving my life."

He chuckled, leaning down to place a kiss to the top of her head. "You got it, kiddo. Don't whoop his ass too hard now."

Liam grunted.

"No promises," his sister called after him.

Jumping in his truck, he turned the engine over and started down the highway toward the county hospital. He knew Liam would protect his baby sister with his life. Since arriving early this morning, the FBI agent had been very concerned over Julie's condition. She assured him she was fine, as did Ryder, but Liam insisted she take it easy. Hence the card game at the table.

He was glad his buddy was there to look after her, since the main portion of his brain was taken up with thoughts of Kayla. The need to see her, touch her, reassure himself she was okay was overwhelming.

Ryder reached the hospital a little after ten in the morning. Not knowing if Kayla would be awake or still sleeping, he cautiously opened the door to her room. She wasn't asleep or awake.

She wasn't there.

The only person in the room was a nurse, stripping the bed. Kayla was nowhere to be seen.

"Excuse me?" he addressed the blonde nurse.

She glanced up, her smile growing broader as she took him in. "Can I help you, sir?"

"Where is the woman who was in here yesterday? Kayla Jenkins."

Her smile faltered. "Are you family?"

He hated that damn question. He understood the need to respect patient's privacy, but family wasn't always flesh and blood. Family was what you made it, and he wanted to make Kayla a part of his.

"I'm Sheriff Ryder," he said, going for another route and pulling out his badge. "I came in with her last night. I need to follow up."

"Oh, well, she left about an hour ago."

"Left?" *What the hell?* "Did she say where she was going?"

The nurse hesitated.

"I still have some questions for her." *Like why did you leave, where are you going, and do you love me, want to stay here, and live the rest of our lives together in blissful happiness?*

"She said she was going home."

To Chicago? Without saying goodbye?

Not if he had anything to say about it.

"I called her a cab. She told me her mother was flying in tonight."

Ryder smelled something foul. Kayla was running again, but not from a murderer this time. She was running from him. The only question now was, why?

"Can you get me the name and number of the cab company you called for her?"

"Of course, Sheriff."

The nurse hurried out of the room. He didn't know why Kayla left without telling him, but he was damn sure going to find out. He loved her.

Yesterday, he thought he lost her forever. No way in hell was he going to lose her today.

****

Kayla unwrapped the plastic covering from her leg. After asking the cab driver to drop her off at the bus station, the man informed her the last bus had left Peak Town for the day. Lack of public transit was a hazard of a small town. Thankfully, they also had silver linings, like the sweet, old Mrs. Bess who the driver informed Kayla often took in wayward travelers down on their luck. Boy, did that describe her to a T. The cabby had dropped her off at Mrs. Bess' door. One look at Kayla hobbling on her crutches and the kind octogenarian whisked her right back to a small cottage in the back yard.

Auntie Bess—as she asked to be called—insisted Kayla take a long, hot shower while she prepared something warm to eat. The doctor instructed her not to get her bandages wet, luckily for her, her generous savior had some plastic wrap on hand so she could enjoy the glorious streams of scalding hot water.

A sigh escaped her, body now blissfully refreshed. Too bad she couldn't say the same for her heart. The poor thing was as bruised and battered as her body right now. Worse.

She had done the right thing. She knew that. So, why did it hurt so much?

Foregoing the hospital scrubs, she put on the fluffy bathrobe hanging in the closet right where Auntie Bess said it would be. A hot meal and the comedy channel sounded like heaven to her right now. Thank goodness for small town kindness. Peak Town had certainly gone far in restoring her faith in humanity.

A knock on the door interrupted her thoughts. For one brief moment, she feared David had come after her again, but he was locked away. He would never hurt her or anyone else ever again.

She shook her head at the silly bit of panic. It had to be Auntie Bess with the promised hot meal. Her stomach rumbled in anticipation. She made her way to the door, hobbling on the crutches the hospital gave her.

Peering through the peephole, she gulped as her heart jumped into her throat. Long, dark hair and warm, brown eyes filled her vision.

A warrior stood at her door. Her warrior.

"Open the door, Kayla."

Undoing the chain, she threw the door open. "Ryder? What are you doing here?"

He glared, moving his way past her into the room. "I might ask you the same question. Why the hell did you leave the hospital without calling me?"

Why was he angry?

"I, um…they released me."

"And so you called a cab to take you to "—he glanced about the room—"Auntie Bess' Home for Wayward Souls?"

Home for Wayward Souls? Did the townspeople really call it that? The cab driver hadn't. Seemed a bit dramatic.

"I was coming back to get you, Kayla. Why didn't you wait?"

"I didn't…"

"What?" He glared when she didn't continue. "You didn't need me anymore now that David is locked up?"

"No!" *How can he think such a thing?* She shifted on the crutches, winching as pain shot up her injured leg.

"Shit, you shouldn't be standing." He gently took her arm, slinging it over his shoulder and carefully sweeping her up into his arms. The crutches fell to the floor, but Ryder simply stepped over them.

He set her down on the bed and stood before her. Dark eyes gazed at her with concern, but his posture was stiff and hard. "You didn't think I deserved a goodbye or at least a damn phone call telling me you were leaving?"

"Ryder, please stop shouting. That's not why I left." She had never seen him this way. Not quite angry, more upset, desperate.

"What the hell am I supposed to think then? David's locked up, you're free to go, and so you just pack up and leave without a word. Your protection detail is over, so you're out of here?"

"No, dammit! That's not it." She was shouting now, too, but she couldn't help it. He had it all wrong, and he looked so hurt by her actions. She was trying to save him from pain, not cause more.

"Then why, Kayla, why? Why did you leave?"

Her heart shattered. "Because I love you, and I only bring pain and death to the people I love." She slumped back on the bed. "David was right. I'm cursed. No one has ever wanted me. I should be alone forever."

Ryder rocked back on his heels as if her words were a forceful blow to his midsection.

Tears streamed down her face. Embarrassed by her outburst, she wiped them away with the sleeve of her robe.

"Oh, sweetheart. Come here." He sat next to her, wrapping his arms around her.

Unable to stop herself, she leaned in, clutching him tight, breathing him in. He smelled so good. She had been afraid she'd never smell his scent again. She shouldn't lean on him, but selfishly, she wanted to keep him.

"Okay, let's take things one at a time." Ryder's deep voice washed over her. "David is a lying dickhead. You *are not* cursed, sweetheart. You had some shitty parent who never deserved you and a wonderful best friend who just took up with the wrong guy. None of that is your fault."

Okay, all true points. She'd give him that. "But he almost killed your sister *and* you, that's my—"

"No," he interrupted harshly. "That is *not* your fault. That is *all* on David Tyler's shoulders, and he *will* pay for what he did. You *saved* my baby sister's life, and mine. I'll be forever grateful to you for that."

She lifted her head, mouth open to argue that Julie wouldn't have needed saving if she didn't put her in harm's way in the first place, but he captured her chin

240

in his hand, staring deeply into her eyes. Those sinfully dark eyes held a world of truth in them. Ryder had never lied to her, not once in the entire—admittedly not long—time she'd known him. Ergo that meant...he had to be telling the truth. His words began to sink in, and the whole situation became clearer. He was right, this wasn't her fault, and by blaming herself she was letting David win.

Stroking her cheek, a smile tilted his lips "Now, about that other thing. The bit about you loving me."

Oh shoot. Had she really blurted that out? She tried to say something, but he placed one finger over her lips, shushing her.

"I gotta say, sweetheart, I'm relieved as hell to hear you say that...because I love you, too."

Blinding white light obscured her vision for a moment. Surely, she hadn't heard him right. He couldn't have actually said the words her heart was aching to hear.

Kayla sniffed, lip trembling. "You do?"

He smiled, and her heart skipped a beat.

"How could I not? You are the strongest, most amazing, beautiful woman I have ever met. I think I fell in love with you the moment I saw you shivering in the snow wearing those ridiculous shoes."

She swatted him playfully. "Hey, I like my shoes."

He hugged her tight. "I do, too, honey. But we have to get you some new ones for day-to-day stuff. They're just not practical up here in the mountains."

"Up here...?"

His palms gently held her face. He leaned down, brushing his lips across hers. "I love you, Kayla. The thought of losing you, in *any* way, is something I can't live with. I need you in my life. Move to Peak Town. Marry me. Be a part of my family, and together, we can make it even bigger."

The words went in her ears, but her heart was so filled with happiness she could barely decipher them.

"You want to marry me? And have a family?" A family. The one thing she always wanted. Only, she never imagined a man as wonderful as Ryder to share it with.

"You already are my family, sweetheart. Family is who you love. And I love you with every ounce of breath I have in me."

More tears flowed from her, but these were tears of happiness. Ryder didn't blame her. He wanted to be a family with her. She wasn't cursed.

He loves me! She couldn't get over it.

"I hope those are happy tears?" he asked with a tentative smile.

She nodded, unable to speak through her joy.

"You'll stay in Peak Town with me? Marry me?"

"Yes," she cried, finally finding her voice. "Yes, yes, yes, to everything."

"Hot damn!"

He scooped her up into his arms, covering her mouth with his in a scorching hot kiss that made her muscles clench in anticipation.

"Please tell me you're naked under this," he murmured from deep in his throat.

She giggled—she was so happy, her heart felt as if it would burst right from her chest. "I just got out of the shower."

Grinning like a kid on Christmas, he laid her gently back down, being cautious of her injuries. Taking off his hat, she spied the small row of stitches on his head. She hated that he'd been hurt, but they were both alive and most importantly, together.

Ryder sank down beside her on the soft pillow top. "About that family? Wanna get started right now?"

She tucked a hand in his shirt, pulling him closer and giving him the answer with her lips, hands, and every other part of her body, which would now and forever be a part of a family. His.

The Ryder family.

It had a nice ring to it.

A word about the author...

RWA® Golden Heart®-nominated author Mariah Ankenman began writing at the tender age of five. Her first book, *George and the Green Glob*, received high praise from her mother. Many years and green glob stories later, Mariah received a playwriting degree from the University of Wyoming. After a few years in Hollywood, working in "the biz," she came home to the beautiful Rocky Mountains. When she's not writing, Mariah loves to read, crochet, and play her ukulele. She loves to hear from readers. You can contact her through her website, Twitter, or Facebook.

www.mariahankenman.com
twitter @MAsbooks
www.facebook.com/mariahankenmanauthor/

Thank you for purchasing
this publication of The Wild Rose Press, Inc.

If you enjoyed the story, we would appreciate your
letting others know by leaving a review.

For other wonderful stories,
please visit our on-line bookstore at
www.thewildrosepress.com.

For questions or more information
contact us at
info@thewildrosepress.com.

The Wild Rose Press, Inc.
www.thewildrosepress.com

Stay current with The Wild Rose Press, Inc.

Like us on Facebook

https://www.facebook.com/TheWildRosePress

And Follow us on Twitter
https://twitter.com/WildRosePress